"Remember?"

Davina gave a jerky nod as she so very vividly recalled how it had all begun.

"A smoky room," Joel murmured, "everyone else at the party having fun. We stood at opposite ends of the room, both leaning against the wall...."

He'd insisted on taking her home.

"Only a few weeks into the New Year," she whispered. "A cold, crisp January night."

"Yes. The night you should have begun your honeymoon. A day that should have been your wedding day...."

Emma Richmond was born during the war in North Kent, England, when, she says, "farms were the norm and freeways nonexistent. My childhood was one of warmth and adventure. Amiable and disorganized, I'm married with three daughters, all of whom have fled the nest—probably out of exasperation! The dog stayed, reluctantly. I'm an avid reader, a compulsive writer and a besotted new granny. I love life and my world of dreams, and all I need to make things complete is a housekeeper—like, yesterday!"

Books by Emma Richmond

HARLEQUIN ROMANCE
3349—LOVE OF MY HEART

HARLEQUIN PRESENTS
1516—UNFAIR ASSUMPTIONS
1582—A STRANGER'S TRUST
1669—MORE THAN A DREAM

A FAMILY CLOSENESS
Emma Richmond

Harlequin Books

TORONTO • NEW YORK • LONDON
AMSTERDAM • PARIS • SYDNEY • HAMBURG
STOCKHOLM • ATHENS • TOKYO • MILAN
MADRID • WARSAW • BUDAPEST • AUCKLAND

ISBN 0-373-03374-5

A FAMILY CLOSENESS

First North American Publication 1995.

This edition published by arrangement with Harlequin Enterprises B.V.

® and TM are trademarks of the publisher. Trademarks indicated with
® are registered in the United States Patent and Trademark Office, the
Canadian Trade Marks Office and in other countries.

Printed in U.S.A.

CHAPTER ONE

'AND although people tend to grow the usual herbs in their gardens for cooking: mint, sage...' Looking up to smile, Davina suddenly froze, stared in disbelief at the man standing at the other end of the room. He was propped against the wall, staring broodingly down into his glass, idly swirling the amber liquid, and then, as though aware of being watched, he looked up. Oh, dear God. Joel Gilman.

Shock rooted her to the spot, then jolted her into panic as she stared round her like a trapped animal searching for an escape route.

'Something is wrong?' Maria queried worriedly. 'You have gone so pale.'

'What?' Jerking her head back to stare at her hostess, her expression quite blank as though she'd forgotten who she was, she hastily pulled herself together. 'No, no, I'm fine.' A palpable lie, but what the hell else could she say? A piece of my past has just jumped up to bite me? 'I have to go!' she exclaimed hurriedly. 'I've just remembered I haven't put some of my notes... Need them for tomorrow's talk. Sorry. Look, I'll see you in the morning.' Aware that she was babbling, unable even to *think* what to say, only knowing that she needed to escape, she dumped her glass on a nearby table, squeezed past a chattering group, hugged the wall, smiled weakly, apologised, and bolted for the door.

The maid was hovering in the hall, and Davina gave her a sickly smile. 'Headache,' she murmured.

'Vina?'

Oh, God. Pretending deafness, heels clicking agitatedly on the polished tiles, she made a dash for the front door—and a strong hand caught her arm, stayed her. Every breath he took seemed a part of hers, the burning mark of each separate pore of each separate finger seemed to dissolve into skin that was suddenly too sensitive, and the warmth of his body so close behind paralysed her.

'Vina?'

No, she wanted to shout. I'm not her, really I'm not. The pressure on her arm increased, and he slowly turned her to face him. Eyes trapped by the blue of his, her body rigid, she just stared at him, fought to pull herself together. 'Joel,' she managed. She sounded as though she was being strangled.

He didn't smile. Anyone else would have smiled, she thought frantically. Anyone else would have allowed her to escape when that was patently what she wanted. Anyone else but Joel.

'I have to go.'

'Not yet.' And his voice was as she remembered it, assured, drawling, the sort of voice that roused violent feelings of antipathy. Black hair still tumbled across the brow above a face that was brooding, moody, almost dissolute. And she wanted to tell him that Byron was dead, that looking like that long-ago poet was old hat. I don't want to be here, she thought.

'It's been a long time.'

'Yes.' Not long enough.

'You look well.'

'Thank you.'

And then he smiled. Not a heartbreaking smile of pure sweetness that one might expect from a man who looked like a fallen angel, but a mere twisting of lips that had grown more cynical than she had ever remembered. He reached out, touched her hair.

'Don't,' she whispered thickly.

'Marmalade hair and amber eyes, like a lynx. I should have painted——'

'Don't. Please don't.'

'No.' He let his hand drop, stepped back. He no longer held his glass. Had he dumped his, as she had?

With a long shudder, she repeated faintly, 'I have to go.'

His smile was knowing, and Davina turned and fled. Extraordinarily grateful for well-oiled hinges, for a handle that turned with ease, she ran down the front steps, and didn't stop running until she reached her rented apartment, didn't relax until she was inside, the door safely bolted behind her. Her heart was beating far too fast, her hands clammy, and there was a sick, churning sensation in her stomach. Joel Gilman. But what was he *doing* here? Why now, after all this time? She hadn't wanted ever to see him again. Hadn't expected she would. And now, in the unlikeliest of places, a small town in Andorra, at a party held by the woman who had arranged her lecture tour, here he was.

Pushing herself upright with arms that shook, she walked across the shadowy lounge, turned on one of the pretty table lamps. She needed a drink. Seeing the bottle of sherry that Maria had given her, a 'welcome to Andorra' present, she twisted off the top, poured a generous measure into a glass with a hand that still shook almost uncontrollably, and sank into the nearby chair. Still feeling sick, disorientated, she reproved herself for a fool. She'd behaved like a frightened virgin—and, heaven knew, virgin was something she wasn't! Some-

thing Joel knew she wasn't! He was the one who'd...
Shutting that thought off at birth, she took a hasty sip
of the sherry. She was articulate, successful, confident—and she'd just run through the streets of Andorra
like a frightened child.

There was the scrape of footsteps outside and she stiffened, staring at her door with fearful eyes, and then
she heard a woman's voice, heard her go into the
apartment next door, and she slumped tiredly. He
wouldn't come. Of course he wouldn't come. Why
should he? She doubted that he wanted to remember
what had happened all those years ago any more than
she did. But *wanting* not to remember didn't necessarily
mean that you didn't.

Finishing her sherry, reassured that he wouldn't come,
desperate to believe it, she went to get ready for bed.
Sleep was a long time coming, perhaps because she kept
trying to shut out memories that didn't want to be shut
out, and yet, when she woke in the morning, to blue
skies and sunshine, her behaviour of the night before
seemed ludicrous. He wouldn't come. Of course he
wouldn't. He'd been as horrified as she had. Don't think
about it. Dismiss him from your mind. Easier said than
done, but she did *try*. And even if he did come, she
argued with herself, would it matter? Really? It had all
happened a long time ago; she was a different person
now—*wasn't* she?

Yet it wouldn't go away, and while she breakfasted,
sorted out her notes, pretended composure there, in the
back of her mind—no, the front of her mind—was Joel
Gilman. The man who... Stop it, Davina. Just stop, she
told herself.

Dressing casually in long tailored shorts and a silk
shirt, striving for normality, she walked along to the

nearby hall where she was to give her talk that evening.
She needed to view the facilities, meet the organisers,
desperately needed to distract her mind, still the frantic
flutter in her breast, and as had been the case so far on
her tour they were kind, charming, enthusiastic. Reassured, the familiarity of her work taking the edge off
her stupid panic, making light of her behaviour the night
before to Maria, apologising, she returned to her
apartment for lunch. Almost able to enjoy the bright
morning, the cheerful greetings of her new, if temporary
neighbours, she forced herself to be calm. She loved this
part of the world—the warmth, the charm, the old that
married seemingly so happily with the new. An independent principality since the Middle Ages and, extraordinary as it might seem, only accessible to the outside
world for the past fifty years. Narrow streets, tiny
hamlets, all enclosed by the towering mountains—and
smuggling, she remembered with a faint smile, had been
regarded for centuries as a national skill.

Feeling a little less fraught, she pushed open the door
to her apartment—and came to a shocked halt. She
stared in disbelief at the tall, black-haired man standing
in her living-room. 'No-o,' she wailed. 'I don't *want* you
here!'

'No,' he agreed, just the faintest twist to his mouth.
Scorn? Mockery?

'Then why are you?' she demanded aggressively, and,
for the moment at least, anger was a weapon she could
use to dispel the fear.

'The door was open.'

'And you just walk into people's houses because the
door is open?'

'No. Ammy was tired.'

'Ammy? There's more than *one* of you?'

His eyes not leaving hers, he gestured behind him and Davina wrenched her gaze away, stared at the small child huddled fast asleep on the sofa, as dark as he, long lashes lying like fans on softly flushed cheeks. A Raggedy Ann doll was clasped safely in one arm. 'She's *yours*?'

'Of course; I'm hardly likely to go carting other people's children around, am I?'

'How would I know? I didn't even know you *had* a child!' And then her eyes widened as realisation hit her, and she stared at him in accusation. 'You had her when...'

'We met? No,' he denied. 'Does that make me less—dislikeable?'

Did it? She had no idea, but she supposed it was marginally better that he'd only cheated on his wife, not a wife *and* child. Disturbed, worried, her knees suddenly weak, she sank down on the chair-arm behind her, continuing to stare at him in bewildered shock. Hands were shoved negligently into his pockets as he rocked back on his heels, returned her gaze with mocking deliberation. 'But what are you *doing* here? Is Celia with you?' she asked stupidly.

'Celia? No, we split up over a year ago.'

'*Again*?' she asked sarcastically before she could stop herself.

'Yes, again.'

Giving him a look of dislike, wondering why on earth he was behaving as though *she* were at fault, she glanced away. Had he arrogantly assumed that she'd be glad to see him? No, he *couldn't* believe that. Returning her eyes to him as though it was some sort of compulsion, she took in the jean-clad legs, the denim shirt. Long and lithe, lean—too lean—a closed face, dark and brooding. Blue eyes, put in with a sooty finger, as the saying went.

He looked Irish, or Spanish, and as far as she knew was neither. He also looked as though he was—waiting. But for what? A smile? To reminisce? And she was having the most desperate trouble in even coming to terms with the fact that he was actually standing in her living-room!

'I don't *want* you here,' she repeated stubbornly.

'I know.'

'Then why are you?'

He gave a slow smile, as though amused by her distress. 'Because Maria said this was where you lived.'

'Don't be so...' Breaking off, she frowned. 'You know Maria?'

'No. I asked her where you were staying.'

'And she *told* you?' Not very sensible; he could have been anybody. 'She didn't say!'

'Didn't she?'

'No!' But why hadn't she? That would have been a natural thing to do, then ask if it had been all right. Still frowning, still staring at him, she pursued, 'And so you thought it would be a good idea just to drop in?'

'No. I needed somewhere to leave Ammy.'

'Somewhere to leave... You're intending to *leave* her with me?' she demanded incredulously. 'I'm not a crèche!'

'I know you're not a crèche,' he agreed with a patience that made her want to scream. 'And I didn't mean leave as in abandon, but leave as in lay down.'

'Well, that's all right, then, isn't it?' she asked derisively, positively yearning to wipe that sadistic smile off his face. 'I'm so glad I was able to be of service! And stop being so confoundedly—complacent! It's not a *game*!' Unable to remain sitting, not knowing *what* to do, how to react, she walked across to the mantelpiece, rearranged the ornaments sitting there. 'And why me?' she demanded agitatedly.

'Because Ammy was tired and you were near by.'

'And that makes it all right?' she swung round to exclaim.

He gave a slow smile. 'Why so agitated, Davina?' he asked softly.

'I'm not agitated! And I don't *believe* you. I really don't *believe* you! I haven't seen you in over four years, no word, no note, noth——' Biting her lip, furious with herself for the stupid slip, she wrenched her gaze back to the shelf.

'Did you *want* a note?' he demanded, as incredulous as she.

'Of course I didn't! But just because we were once...'

'Intimate?' he asked helpfully. 'Don't like to be reminded, Vina?'

'Don't call me that! And no, I don't. It's hardly something to be proud of.'

'It happened,' he shrugged.

'Yes.' An overwhelming passion that had transcended thought, honour, and she still felt ashamed—no, mortified, because she had been the instigator. Had deliberately—seduced, she supposed. At a time when she'd been feeling very vulnerable, one touch had ignited them both. Not looking at him, she stared at the sleeping child, and asked almost indifferently, a pretend indifference, because whatever else this man generated it was not indifference, 'What are you doing in Andorra anyway?'

'A commission.'

As economical with words as he'd once been with the truth. 'Then why bring—Ammy, was it?'

'Yes. Amaryllis. She didn't want to be left.'

'Didn't want to be...' Astonished, she exclaimed, 'She's what? Three? Four? And *she* dictates the rules? You *have* changed! The Joel I once knew never gave in to anybody, especially if they were female.'

'I gave in to you,' he pointed out softly.

Her cheeks flaming, hating him for the reminder of something she preferred to forget, the sheer shame and embarrassment of it, she taunted raggedly, 'And do you accommodate all the women who throw themselves at your head?'

'No,' he denied mildly.

'Then why me?'

'Perhaps because I saw desperation instead of desire? And you didn't *know* me—any more than you do now.' Glancing at his sleeping daughter, he gave a faint smile. 'She does.' And for the first time since she'd walked through the door his dark blue eyes glinted with genuine amusement. 'She can wrap me round her little finger,' he confessed. Almost a matter for pride.

Hearing the note of love in his voice, Davina looked away, a lump in her throat. The only person he'd ever loved? Was capable of loving? Certainly she'd never heard that particular note in his voice when he'd spoken to herself, never heard it when he'd spoken of his wife.

'You got custody?'

'No, but I get to see her whenever I want.' That mocking smile twisting his mouth again, he added softly, 'And, even more importantly, she gets to see me whenever *she* wants. That sets your mind at rest, does it?'

Refusing to be drawn, she commented stiffly, 'She looks like you.'

'Yes.'

And if things had been different, Ammy might have been her own child. But things hadn't been different, yet Joel as a father seemed—inconceivable.

'Can I use your phone?' he asked casually.

'I don't have one.'

'Don't *have* one?'

'No! And there's no need to sound so incredulous— although, had I known I was to get all these unwelcome visitors, naturally I'd have had one put in! There's a public one at the end of the road,' she added grudgingly.

He nodded, turned away. 'I won't be long.'

'You're going *now*?' she demanded in astonishment.

'I'll only be five minutes!'

'And supposing she wakes?'

'She won't.'

'But supposing she does? And don't sigh at me!'

'Then we'll just have to hope she doesn't take a dislike to you, won't we?'

'Dislike? I was thinking more along the lines of her being frightened!'

'She wouldn't be; she knows I wouldn't leave her anywhere unsafe.'

'Oh, *what* a bright child!'

Unexpectedly, he grinned. 'Just like her father.'

'That isn't what I meant.'

'I know. Coffee?'

And that was it? Four years wiped away as though they'd never been? Not knowing what else to do, say, she walked across to the kitchen. Closing the door behind her, leaning back against it, she forced herself to acknowledge that Joel Gilman—*the* Joel Gilman—was in her home, in the flesh, that he had looked her up because he wanted somewhere to leave his child, not because of her, not because of what had happened, but because he needed a babysitter! And she didn't know how she felt. Shocked, confused, disturbed. Their union all those years ago had been violent, passionate, a compulsion almost, but not loving. They'd used each other. Not clinically, not calculatingly, but both had had a need for closeness, warmth. She wasn't sure she had ever liked him, only been affected by him, aroused by him. Unable to forget him. And the tension was still there, the sexual awareness, on both sides, despite his mockery and her over-reaction, and only now could she honestly admit, seeing him again, that no man had ever made her feel as he had. Satiated. There was a darkness in his soul...cynicism and self-interest governed his actions, and yet... Feeling the pressure against the door at her back, she moved away, went to fill the percolator. And after her knee-jerk reaction of last night, of just now, she determined that he would not be allowed to rout her again. Must not—because her continued aggression might begin to make him wonder, and she most definitely didn't want that.

'How's your mother?' she asked without turning. That was a safe topic, wasn't it? She knew about his mother. Natalie Gilman. Ageing actress. Knew about other areas of his life, because he was forever in the tabloids, one escapade after another. Wine, women, and ridiculous stunts that he was lucky hadn't killed him.

'As ever.'

'Then why didn't you leave Ammy with her?'

'I told you, I wanted Ammy with me, and even if I hadn't she wouldn't have *wanted* to have Ammy left with her. She's not maternal.'

'Don't be ridiculous. She had you.'

'Precisely. She doesn't like children.'

Turning only her head, she asked in pardonable astonishment, 'And what does that mean?'

'Whatever you want it to.'

'Stop playing games. She must have liked you!'

He shook his head.

'Oh, come on...' Searching his face, seeing only the sardonic certainty that he was right, and unbearably conscious of his presence, annoyed with herself for feeling—unsettled, unsure, and determined to keep a large amount of space between them, she busied herself getting out cups. 'Will Ammy have a drink when she wakes?' she asked aloofly.

'Juice if you have it.'

She nodded and, unbearably aware of the fact that he was watching her closely, went to get the juice from the fridge, trying not to fumble, trying for casual interest. What she should have tried for in the first place. 'What did Maria tell you?'

'Only that you were here to give a talk on herbs...' With an abrupt laugh, he asked, 'What on earth made you take *that* up?'

Furious that anyone—no, not anyone, *he*—should disparage something she passionately believed in, she turned to face him, the juice carton clasped in her arms. 'I took it up because I believe alternative medicine has a place in the scheme of things. Believe that it helps. Where drugs——'

'OK, OK, spare me the lecture,' he murmured, his hands held out placatingly. 'I was only curious. It just didn't seem the sort of thing you'd be interested in, that's all.'

'And why not?' she demanded defensively.

He shrugged, and she wondered if perhaps he was as reluctant as she to rake over old coals. In which case, why not avoid her as she'd always tried to avoid him? Why turn up in her apartment with the flimsiest excuse she'd ever heard? Not wanting even to *consider* what ulterior motive he might have, she turned away. Collecting a glass, she carefully poured the juice. 'What were you doing at the party?'

'Socialising?'

Her mouth tight, expression stony, she replaced the juice in the fridge.

'I came out to see Martin Devera,' he explained eventually. 'He wants me to paint his portrait.'

'And he was at the party, was he?' she asked sarcastically.

'No.'

'But you saw me, and you calculatingly——'

'Not calculatingly,' he denied quietly. 'I was on my way to see him this morning. Ammy was tired...' Leaving the sentence hanging, he turned away.

'And good old Davina lived near by,' she completed for him. Angry without really knowing why, finding spoons, sugar, cream, she thumped them on the surface. 'Just because ... That doesn't give you the right ... I'm not here to be used!'

'The way you once used me?' he asked softly.

A spoon clenched in her hand, she whirled to face him. 'I did not!'

'No?'

'No. We used each other,' she muttered.

'Did we? Funny, I thought it was an overwhelming attraction.'

'No, you didn't!' she denied vehemenently. 'You wanted sex!'

'*You* wanted sex,' he corrected mildly, 'as an act of revenge. And you can't forget it, can you?'

'Of course I can!'

His blue eyes disconcertingly direct, he stared at her for long, long moments. 'I can't,' he confessed, barely loud enough for her to hear.

Startled, her own eyes wide, her heart-rate suddenly slowing, a heavy thud that beat in her ears, she whispered, 'What?'

'I——'

'Don't,' she broke in almost agitatedly. 'Don't say...'

He gave a cynical smile, and then his face closed, grew moody again. Wandering over to look through the window, Davina let out a little puff of relief. He mustn't... It was stupid—and couldn't possibly be true. Anyway, she had her own life now. A successful life. Fulfilled! Do you, Davina? Do you really? she asked herself. And if he couldn't forget, why had he never contacted her?

'You think I was proud of what happened?' he asked quietly.

'No,' she breathed thickly.

'It wasn't intended. I hadn't sought you out...' No, she was the one who'd done that. 'It just—happened. Or so I thought. Then.'

'Don't,' she repeated quickly. 'And I explained that it was... that I...'

'So you did. Were brutally direct, in fact. Woke me in the morning, told me that you'd been using me to punish your ex-lover...'

'Fiancé,' she corrected him stupidly, as though it mattered. He'd stared at her that morning, cold and withdrawn, then blazingly savage in his contempt—because she had been unable to explain that her behaviour was the result of self-disgust, a humiliating awareness that he must think her cheap, a tramp. And so he'd gone,

leaving behind him an anguished and frightened little
girl—an even more frightened little girl when she'd discovered she was pregnant. She could still clearly recall
the despair, and had thought in her foolishness, when
the memory of that night had become more vivid, instead of less, that she could explain to him, that he would
understand—only to find that he was still with his wife.
Or had gone back to her, if he was to be believed. And
so he had never known. And now never would. A few
weeks later, she had miscarried, and that had seemed
like just another betrayal.

'Davina?'

Blinking, she straightened, tried to look attentive.

'I needed some help, that's all. A favour, for old times'
sake, and the funny thing is you're one of the few people
that I really trust. You don't want, or expect, anything
of me. Do you?'

'No.'

'And so I feel—safe with you.' Self-mockery twisting
his mouth, he glanced around. 'Amusing, huh?'

'No.' It wasn't amusing at all; neither was she sure
she believed him; he was a devious devil—or so everyone
said. In all honesty, apart from their brief—liaison—all
she knew about him had been culled from others.
Hearsay, the tabloids, and heaven knew his reputation
preceded him everywhere he went, and yet she had
sometimes wondered if his agent didn't promote his difficult behaviour, his notoriety, womanising, because it
was good for business. Although there was no denying
that he *was* difficult...moody, passionate, one of the
most gifted of modern painters; perhaps such brilliance
had to be balanced by a down side.

But a favour? For old times' sake? When she had deliberately alienated him? 'You never got in...' Biting

her lip, because she hadn't meant to say that, she stared
down at the spoon she was unconsciously trying to bend.

'Touch? No. Do you ever see him?' he asked casually.

'Paul? No.'

'He was a fool.'

'No,' she denied. 'He was in love.' She could admit
it now, accept it now, had for a long time. Forgive, because there was no escaping the fact that if Jenny had
made Paul feel one-tenth of what Joel had made her
feel, then admittedly, in retrospect, there hadn't been a
choice.

'I doubt I'd be so generous.'

No, she doubted it too.

'Running off with your best friend. Ditched at the
altar...'

'It was a long time ago.'

'Yes. A long time ago. And if——'

'Don't.' Hearing the coffee bubbling behind her, she
turned off the heat, carefully poured it into two cups.
'Did Celia leave you because——?'

'Of other women?' he drawled. He sounded amused.
'No. And she didn't leave me; it was a mutual agreement.'
Taking his coffee, he gave her a wry smile. 'You never
met her, did you?'

'No.' She didn't even know what she looked like.
Didn't want to know.

'You'd probably have liked her. *I* liked her, but not
as a—partner. We should never have lived together, of
course, n——'

'Then why did you?' And why not say married? Why
living together? Because he hadn't felt married?

Staring down into his cup, he explained slowly, 'I was
an up-and-coming young painter—she liked doing good
works...' With a fleeting smile, as though there was a

memory there that pleased him, he glanced up, smiled more naturally. 'Whoever knows why we do things?'

'A case of it seemed like a good idea at the time?'

'Mmm. Celia liked lame ducks...'

'Joel!' she protested. 'You're the least likely lame duck I've ever met!'

Laughter spilled into his eyes, etched the corner of his mouth. 'Mmm,' he agreed, 'but she yearned to be someone's patron.'

'And when you were no longer in need of one?'

'Something like that,' he agreed. 'Things had been rocky for some time...'

'You told me you were separated,' she accused.

'We were——'

'No, you weren't! Don't lie!'

His face darkened, became frighteningly cold. 'I do not lie, Davina. Ever. Not then, not now, and the fact that you choose to interpret events to suit yourself is no one's problem but your own. If it minimises your own guilt——'

'I did not feel guilty!'

'Then you should have done,' he reproved quietly.

Flushing, she looked quickly down, because she had felt guilty. Still did.

'We *had* split up,' he continued, 'but I did not tell you that we never saw each other, and that day, that one particular day, we'd had an almighty row. She'd come round to accuse me of something or other, I'd already been in a foul mood because a commission I was doing wouldn't go right, and the whole thing escalated out of all proportion. I stormed off to that party—and there you were...'

'Yes,' she agreed quickly, because she did not, positively did not want a post-mortem on what had hap-

pened at that party. 'And then you got back together.'
Because he'd still loved Celia, because his liaison with
Davina had meant nothing.

'Yes.'

'Did she know? About me?'

'Not then. You think I advertised it?'

'No, of course I don't. But she knows now?'

'Knows there was someone, not who it was.'

'And were there other...? Sorry, none of my business.'

He gave a slight smile, stared down into his cup. 'No,
and no. Not then, anyway. We had Ammy, made a con-
certed effort, but it wasn't working; she was miserable,
I was bloody-minded as only I can be, and so we
eventually separated. It was entirely amicable. A relief
to us both. We're even quite good friends.'

How very glib. A practised explanation—and maybe
he didn't lie, but neither, she suspected, was he telling
the whole truth. 'Then if you're such good friends,
couldn't you have left Ammy with her?'

'Could. Didn't want to. Anyway, she was off on a trip
somewhere, and although I'm cynical about everyone's
motives, including my own, in as much as I'm capable
of loving anyone I do love Ammy. I even enjoy her
company.'

'Good.' What else could she say? Deciding that the
kitchen was becoming claustrophobic, she led the way
back to the lounge—and was unbearably aware of him
at her back. His closeness, his magnetism, the way that
everything faded when he was around—and she still
didn't understand why that should be. He gave very little
of himself away, his voice always held a note of unin-
terest, as though he cared very little for anyone, including himself. She knew very well that he never put
himself out for anyone. Unutterably selfish—except,

presumably, where his daughter was concerned. So why *had* he sought her out?

And because words were needed, because they provided a barrier, the only barrier she could produce, she murmured, 'I've read about you from time to time.'

'Nothing good, I dare say.'

'No. Except for your work, of course.'

'Of course.'

Glancing back at him, seeing the cynicism that twisted his mouth, she quickened her step, wanted to run, hide. Wanted the day to begin again, differently.

Ammy was sitting up on the sofa, her raggedy doll held on her lap, and Davina was forced to appear normal, or try to. A pretty little girl, and she looked patient, as though she was used to waiting around endlessly in strange places for her father. Perhaps she was. Davina smiled at her, and blue eyes, so very like Joel's, silently weighed her up.

'Dolly awake now,' she announced.

'Oh, right. Did she have a nice sleep?'

'Yes.' She looked at her father. Waited.

He smiled at her, then glanced at Davina. 'Five minutes?'

'Joel...'

He sighed.

'She doesn't even *know* me!' she protested, automatically keeping her voice low.

'She knows me, knows I wouldn't leave her anywhere she'd be unhappy.'

'What? At four years old?'

'Three. And a half,' he added, as though six months made all the difference. Made it all right.

'That's not the point!'

'Then what is?'

'She doesn't *know* me,' she insisted. 'And *I* don't know anything about children!'

'Then now's your chance to learn,' he said with arrogant impatience.

'*Joel*, I don't *want* to learn!'

'Then I'll take her with me.'

'To the phone box?'

'No, to see Devera.'

Knowing she was arguing for argument's sake, she muttered, 'He might not like children.'

'Then he'll have to learn, won't he? If he wants me to paint his portrait.'

'Don't be so...' Glancing at the little girl, she bit back what she was about to say, although she knew very well that she'd be unable to hear their low-voiced conversation. 'And your patience didn't last long, did it?' she sneered. 'Anyway, you can't go dragging her round like an unwanted parce——' Breaking off, because the look he gave her was positively dangerous, she backed up when he moved towards her.

'Don't *ever* tell me how to treat my daughter. Does she look unhappy?' he demanded.

'No,' she muttered.

'Neglected?'

'No.' And she didn't; she looked, clean, well cared for. 'But that doesn't mean ... And you shouldn't shout in front of her.'

'She's used to shouting. She thinks it's the normal way to behave.'

'Well, that's hardly a laudable boast!'

He grinned tightly, almost savagely, and then he relaxed, walked across to ruffle Ammy's hair. 'Yes?' he persuaded.

'I have to go out.'

'Davina! I'll be five minutes!'

'Make sure you are. I can't be late...'

'For your lecture, yes, about herbs—I know.'

'Talk,' she corrected him primly. 'I don't lecture. And don't shout at me. I'm doing you a *favour.*'

'Are you?' he asked softly.

'Yes!'

Turning his attention to his daughter, he smiled. A genuine smile, full of love and affection. 'Yes?' he asked softly.

Ammy looked worried for a moment, glanced at Davina, then back to her father. 'Back soon,' she said with a funny little nod, as though it was something that was always said, and Davina found that there was a little lump in her throat.

'Back soon,' he softly confirmed.

'Won't be long,' she added with a little shake of her head that was endearingly comical.

'No.'

'Just up the road.'

'Yes.'

'Be good,' she nodded.

'Yes.' Glancing at Davina, no guile now in his expression, no anger, he said softly, 'Thanks. I'll be as quick as I can.'

Not wanting him to have it all his own way, she muttered, 'Make sure you are.'

He laughed, bent to kiss Ammy, gave Davina a wicked grin, and if she hadn't taken a hasty step backwards would probably have kissed *her,* and left.

Feeling wrung out, shaken, she sank down beside Ammy, forced herself to smile. 'What's dolly's name?'

'Dolly.'

With a helpless laugh, she asked, 'Would you like some juice?'

When five minutes had stretched to ten, then to twenty, Davina made lunch for them both, and they washed up together with Ammy standing on a chair, playing with the bubbles, and feelings that she'd unconsciously repressed, or perhaps hadn't even known she had, churned inside Davina, hurting her. To marry, have children, a family closeness. Things she had wanted, things she had thought within her grasp. Where had the years gone? she wondered. Why had there been no other man to fill that empty space?

After she'd helped the little girl down, loving the feel of her, the innocence, they returned to the lounge. Finding an empty shoe-box to make Dolly a bed, leaving Ammy to play contentedly on the floor, she sat and watched her, remembered, allowed it all to flood back. That fateful day when she had first met Joel. The humiliation, the hurt of being jilted, of Paul going off with her best friend just weeks before the wedding. So much anguish, heart-searching, as though it were her fault for not being loving enough, special enough, and if she'd not been quite suicidal then she had been something close to it. She'd felt worthless, she remembered, a non-person, and if well-meaning friends hadn't dragged her along to that fateful party...

'Cuddle.'

Blinking, she stared at Ammy, who stood before her, arms held out. 'Cuddle?' With a smile that felt wretched, full of pain, she lifted the little girl on to her lap, held the soft, warm body against her, rested her chin on her hair. Joel's daughter—who could have been her own. 'Does Dolly want a cuddle too?' And if her voice was a little bit husky, then thankfully Ammy was too young to notice.

'No. Dolly 'sleep.'

'OK.'

Warm arms were wrapped round her neck, a face pressed briefly to hers, and, as though reassured, Ammy climbed down, smiled, and went back to playing with Dolly, talking to her, mimicking her father presumably, and her mother, using phrases they said to her.

She had known it was wrong, and hadn't cared... No, that wasn't strictly true; she had cared, and part of her had been horrified at her behaviour, but the other part—the not so nice part—had been glad, because she had wanted to punish someone, anyone, for what had been done to her. And he had been so unbelievably attractive, sexy, even in the foul mood he'd been in that day, that brooding, dark side of him that both attracted and repelled. And he'd looked exactly what he was—moody, difficult, artistic—and she had thought then that he didn't give a damn about anybody, or anything. She'd been jilted, he'd had a row with his supposedly ex-wife, and both were feeling absolutely bloody. Two souls in torment who had gravitated towards each other, become passionately entwined, and then parted. It had started out as an act of revenge, and turned into something that had shaken her rigid. And it frightened her, had always frightened her, that loss of control, that side of her she hadn't known existed.

And now he was back, however briefly, and she had to cope with that. She was no longer twenty-two, no longer naïve, no longer hurt. She was competent, successful, and if not exactly wealthy, then she had enough for her needs. More than enough. She had a lifestyle she enjoyed: she travelled extensively for material for her books on alternative remedies, was happy, contented. She had thought herself fulfilled, lucky—had told herself so—and almost believed it. But now, remembering the feel of Ammy's warm little body, the generous hug, she knew there was an area of her life that needed to be filled. Wanted to be filled. And she didn't know what the hell she was going to do about it. Or about Joel. Part of her wanted him to go out of her life as quickly as he had entered it—and the other part remembered all too clearly how he had made her feel. How he could probably still make her feel, given half a chance. And that frightened her even more because to him this was a chance encounter. He'd seen her and no doubt thought it would be amusing to—what? Continue where they had left off? Or punish her for the things she had once said, done?

Hearing a sound in the small courtyard outside, she looked up, glanced at her watch, and deliberately arranged her face into lines of disapproval.

Ammy beamed, hopped to her feet and went to wait at the door. 'Daddy,' she said happily.

As Davina watched the handle turn, there was a sick excitement in her stomach, a fluttering along her nerves that she tried desperately to suppress.

'I know, I know,' he forestalled her, 'I'm sorry. Have you ever tried using a public phone here?'

'Yes.'

He gave her a long look, then a wry smile. 'And never had any trouble,' he murmured as he scooped Ammy up into his arms.

'No.' Not strictly true, but she didn't intend to tell him that.

He stared at her over his daughter's head, his eyes sending a message that she did not understand, and Davina swallowed nervously, got to her feet.

'She's had some lunch.'

He nodded.

'You eventually got through?'

'No, I went round to his house. I thought it would be quicker.'

'I see. And how did it go?'

'It didn't.'

'Didn't?' she echoed, confused.

'No.' Planting a kiss on his daughter's hair, he set her down, shoved his hands into his jean pockets, leaned back against the door, continued to watch her broodingly. And as Ammy went back to playing with her doll he added quietly, 'I couldn't concentrate.'

Nervous, wary, feeling the tension that emanated from him, unable to tear her eyes from his, she whispered, 'Why?'

'You know why.'

'No. No, I don't.'

He shrugged, pushed himself upright. 'Anyway, he wanted to dictate terms.'

'And no one's allowed to dictate terms?'

'No. I do it how I want it or I don't do it at all.'

'Arrogant.'

'Yes, but then I *am* arrogant, aren't I?' he asked softly as he walked towards her.

With nowhere to retreat immediately, because the sofa was behind her, and not wanting to run round the end like a frightened child, she lifted her chin, waited, silently warned him off—but excitement was lacing along her nerve-endings and, no matter how much she might wish him elsewhere, she could not pretend indifference. She felt as she had felt once before that overpowering chemistry that robbed the mind of sense. That overwhelming feeling of—want. Feelings she had never felt for any other man she had ever met.

He stood in front of her, eyes roving over her face, lingering on her mouth, and she felt hot, shivery. 'Don't,' she breathed. 'Please don't do this to me.'

'I want you.'

'No.'

'Yes. I want to taste you, feel you...'

'No.' And her voice sounded as though it was being strained through wire. 'You can't play tit for tat.'

'Can't I?'

'No. I'm engaged,' she blurted.

'Ditch him.'

'I don't *want* to ditch him. I happen to be in *love* with him.'

'Doesn't exist,' he denied.

'Doesn't exist for you,' she corrected him desperately.

'No. Just sensation, feeling—like this.' Reaching out, he trailed one finger down her cheek, then smiled mirthlessly when she flinched. 'You're afraid of me.'

'No. And I have to go and get ready.'

'It's only three. Hours yet. I think about it a lot,' he murmured throatily as his eyes returned to her mouth. 'Lick your lips,' he ordered.

Her throat blocked, her breathing almost suspended, she croaked a denial. 'No.'

CHAPTER TWO

'THEN I will.' Leaning forward, Joel ran his tongue along her defiantly closed lips, and she shuddered.

There was a pain in Davina's stomach, a moistness inside, and she clenched her hands tight. The scent of his skin was in her nostrils, she felt his warmth, without the need to touch, and she knew by the expression in his eyes, his whole body language, that he felt the same. Did her perfume drift in his mind? The scent of her newly washed hair?

'In my dark moments,' he murmured thickly, 'when I'm drinking too much, I remember what happened. The—power of it, and it spoilt me...'

'Don't,' she protested. Putting out a hand to ward him off, she edged sideways, only to have him easily block her move. He used no force—he didn't need to. 'Ammy's watching,' she said desperately.

'No, she isn't.'

He didn't even glance round, didn't need to because they both knew she was absorbed in playing with her doll. 'Or is she used to this?' she taunted raggedly. 'Her father seducing strange women...'

'You aren't strange—and don't be bitchy.'

Closing her eyes in defeat, she pleaded again, 'Please don't do this.'

'Are you really engaged?'

'Yes,' she lied. And he stepped back, released her. Surprised, grateful, her lovely eyes a mixture of fear and desire, she jerked a much needed breath into her lungs, and hurried towards the door. Racing to the bathroom, she locked herself in. Her breath was coming in shuddering gasps and she felt sick. Sick of herself, sick of his power—and for two pins she would have buried herself in his embrace. Her legs unsteady, she moved across to the sink, clutched the white porcelain, stared at her shocked face in the mirror. Her amber eyes looked darker, haunted.

'Vina?'

'Go away,' she groaned.

'Ammy wants to use the loo.'

Oh, God. Returning to the door, she unlocked it, stood aside to let them both in, watched with hungry eyes as he helped his daughter, held her while she washed her hands, then carefully dried them. And then, finally, he looked at her. 'I'm sorry,' he apologised quietly.

She nodded, didn't think herself capable of speech.

'We'll wait for you in the lounge.'

She nodded again, thankfully closed the door behind them. That was what made him so dangerous. That ability to switch from arrogance to gentleness in seconds, to undermine moods that he'd created. He's just a man, she told herself. No better, no worse, no different... Oh, don't be so stupid! If he were like any other man you wouldn't be hiding in the bathroom shaking as though you had a fever!

He could destroy her—and the awful, the terrible thing was that she *wanted* it. Him. And had she really forgotten the intensity of their feelings for each other? Buried it so successfully inside that she'd been able to dismiss it? Because she'd been ashamed? No, she admitted honestly, it hadn't been shame that had made her banish it from her mind, not entirely. It had been the knowledge that she could not have him. Not at the time, because she had been too raw from Paul's rejection, but later, when the pain of being jilted had gone—yes, then. And had she naïvely believed that one man's love-making was much like another's? That it would have been like that with Paul? Yes, she had, until she had met Paul again just before she had discovered she was pregnant, and known, without his even touching her, that it would not be so. *That* was when the enormity of it had overwhelmed her.

She hadn't forgotten it—of course she hadn't; she had merely tried to bury it along with her shameful be-haviour, but in nearly five years had she really not re-membered the sheer animal magnetism of the man? Or was he one of those people you had to see in order to feel? No, she had also buried it because it had frightened her. As it still frightened her. Normal, well-adjusted people didn't behave like that. They weren't *intense*. Not like that: savagery barely leashed. Not in *Surrey* they weren't. Not where she lived.

Aren't they? And how would you know? she asked herself. Ever since he went back to his wife, you've been burying your head in the sand, afraid of being rejected again. Rejecting every man that ever comes near you. And now you want what he's unable to give. Love. Warmth, caring, closeness, a family, a little girl like Ammy, and that's just so funny, tragically so, because all he wants is your body. And why? Because I represent a challenge? Because I used him all those years ago and he now wants to use me? Or is it just—opportunity? Or teasing? she suddenly wondered. He's seen my vulner-ability, and decided to use it? Oh, does it really matter what it is, Davina? she asked herself impatiently. You're not a child! You don't intend to have anything to do with him, so does it really matter what game he's playing?

Yet despite her determination she deliberately lingered over getting ready so that she wouldn't have to be alone with him again. Forced silly, wayward emotions under control, told herself they had only escaped because he'd surprised her, come upon her without warning. Well, she wouldn't be caught that way twice. She was in control now. Her sensible head firmly on, and clad in her businesslike suit, a suit that enhanced every curve, flowed almost lovingly over her hips, her hair tied tidily back, she checked her briefcase, closed it with a determined snap, took a deep breath, and walked into the lounge.

Joel was lying on the floor, long, jean-clad legs crossed at the ankle, shirt-sleeves rolled up, Ammy sitting astride his back, watching over his shoulder as he carefully fed Dolly her bottle, gently scolded her for drinking too fast—and Davina's firmly suppressed emotions spiralled out of control. His thick dark hair was ruffled, untidy, his strong face relaxed.

He turned his head, gave her an engaging grin, a grin she hadn't known him capable of, and said solemnly, 'Dolly's being very naughty.'

'Is she?' she asked helplessly.

'Yes. So she'll have to go to sleep without her bottle.'

'Sleep without her bottle,' Ammy echoed equally solemnly, accompanied, as ever, by the little nod.

Reaching back, Joel grasped Ammy's hands, hauled her flat, got to his knees, then his feet, straightened with a groan, and carefully lowered his daughter to the floor. 'You're getting heavy, Moppet.'

'Heavy,' she agreed with a grin, and she looked up at her father with such an expression of adoration on her small face that Davina felt like crying. Ammy had the right to look at him so. Davina did not have—nor thought she had ever needed to, until now.

'Where's the lecture being held?'

'What? Oh, not far. Round the corner, in fact; that's why I took this apartment.'

'Then we'll walk with you. How many have you given?'

'Three so far. In Spain. León, Burgos, Lleida. Another tonight...'

'And then where? Back home?'

'Yes.'

He nodded, gave her an amused look, and as Ammy bent to collect up her doll he whispered wickedly, 'Very good. You sound almost normal.'

'I am normal,' she argued defiantly. 'I've also changed. I'm no longer the green girl you once knew.'

'Mmm,' he agreed with wicked provocation, 'I can see how you've changed. And in all the right places too.'

'Thank you,' she accepted with sweet derision, and he laughed. Sounded delighted. And from when he'd arrived, moody and brooding, he now looked relaxed, happy, mischievously pleased with himself.

'Where are you staying?' she asked aloofly.

'The Grand,' he murmured with an amused quirk. 'Where else?'

Where else indeed? He liked, and expected, the best. 'Very nice,' she commented with only marginal sarcasm.

'We think so, don't we, Ammy?'

Ammy smiled.

'They also have a babysitting service.'

'Really? How convenient.'

'But only at night.'

With a little movement of her head to indicate that she'd heard, but wasn't really interested, she opened the door, allowed them through, then closed and, this time, locked it. Leading the way across the tiled courtyard, her high heels tapping importantly, she held open the outer gate, closed it firmly until the latch clicked, and began to walk along the quiet little cul-de-sac.

'How long does the lecture last?'

'Talk,' she corrected. 'I talk for about an hour, and——'

'In French? Spanish? I'm impressed.'

'No,' she denied crossly, 'I have an interpreter. And then anyone who wants to asks questions. And stop laughing! It's not remotely funny!'

'Of course it isn't,' he soothed. 'Not funny at all. You're a very important lady, articulate, knowledge-able—and don't shout in front of my daughter.'

'Don't . . . ? You . . .' With a fulminating glance, she swept on. Reaching the hall where she was to give her talk, she pushed inside without further acknowledge-ment of him. Well, that put him in his place, Davina! she told herself. Disgusted with herself, she hurried across to her waiting hosts. She felt all trembly inside, and hardly composed enough to give a talk! On anything!

Moving into the inner hall, taking deep breaths to calm herself, she mounted the rostrum, smiled at the group before her, and familiarity took over. Joel pushed firmly to the back of her mind, she spoke eloquently, easily on her subject, a subject she believed whole-heartedly in. She explained how she had begun, with the desire to help ease her mother's arthritis, reading, learning all she could, garnering other information along the way, until, eventually, she had decided to write a book about it. And then another book because there was simply too much material to put in just one. Fascinated, intrigued by the vast number of herbal remedies, she had found her interest extending to other areas of homeopathy, and everything had just snowballed. With a warm smile, she went on to say that she was here not only to talk about her own discoveries but also to learn, find out what *they* used, discover if there were similar plants growing here, similar uses.

Inviting questions, she caught a movement from the corner of her eye. Automatically turning in that direction, and seeing the outer door edge open, she smiled, ready to wait until the latecomer was seated, and then froze, because the latecomer was Joel.

Her smile dying, she glared at him, and of course, naturally, everyone turned to look, was curious to see the cause of such fury. Dragging her eyes away from him, but still aware in the periphery of her vision that he leaned against the wall, arms folded across his chest, a copy of her book held in one hand, an expression of false interest on his face, she forced herself to go on with the meeting, make notes about their own ideas, remedies that were put forward.

How she got through it all without betraying herself she never knew, but she *did* get through it, and when all questions had been exhausted, when she had patiently answered all that she was asked, she walked across to where he still leaned by the door.

'You did that on purpose,' she accused him.

His finely marked eyebrows rose in simulated surprise. 'I came to listen to you talk,' he argued mildly.

'No, you didn't! You came to make me look a fool!'

His mouth twisted. 'No one else can make you look a fool. Only *you* can do that. And you didn't—until now,' he added tauntingly. Straightening, he took her arm, smiled at those still hovering, and steered her outside.

'I thought we would go back to the hotel, have a drink...'

'Oh, did you?' she asked furiously as she wrenched her arm out of his hold.

'I also,' he continued mildly, 'need to check on Ammy.'

'Then go and check on her!'

He caught her arm again as she swung away, halted her, brought her back to face him. 'It happened,' he said softly. 'It won't go away. So don't you think it would be best to talk about it? Try to come to terms with it?'

'Best?' she exclaimed in astonishment. 'Best for whom?' Glaring at him, agitated all over again, angry, she shook her head. 'No, I do not think it best! And I came to terms with it a long time ago!'

'Did you?'

'Yes!' she hissed. '*You* seem to be the one who hasn't done so!'

'Oh, but I have,' he said softly.

'Then why are you pursuing me? Because you arrogantly assume I didn't mean to...' She bit her lip, furious with herself for giving him ammunition, insights...

'Reject me?' he queried even more softly. 'Use me for revenge?'

'No! You're twisting things! I didn't...'

'Mean it?'

'Yes! No! Oh, stop it! Stop doing this to me!'

'I wasn't aware I was doing anything,' he returned mildly, and with unwarranted arrogance. 'And as you seem to be labouring under so many misapprehensions, I do feel it would be best to discuss them. And anyone would think, the way you're behaving, that I'm the only man who's ever touched you, which is patently absurd.'

'Patently!' she agreed derisively—and untruthfully.

'So you can either come quietly or you can come protestingly, but you will come.'

'No, I won't, and you can't make me!'

'Can't? Or won't?' he asked tauntingly, and when she didn't answer, merely glared impotently at him, he smiled again. 'I both can and will. And how would it look, do you think, for the famous Davina Reynolds to be carried kicking and screaming into the Grand Hotel?'

'I hate you!'

'Yes,' he agreed quietly, 'I imagine you do.'

Startled, she just stared at him. She opened her mouth, then closed it again because what could she say? That she didn't? And what good would that do her? But why didn't he hate her? Or did he?

'Come on,' he encouraged.

'Why?' she demanded, sounding far more perplexed than she wanted. '*Why* this insistence?'

'Because we're strangers in a strange land?' he asked with an odd smile. 'Because we're old—friends?' Linking his hand more comfortably in her elbow, he turned her, urged her along the narrow street. 'Do you think I didn't feel some measure of guilt for what happened?'

'You didn't do anything that——' Breaking off, she bit her lip.

'That you didn't ask for?'

'Yes. I was...'

'I know. You really don't need to defend yourself to me. Not now, anyway. Admittedly, I was pretty angry at the time.'

Yes. Savage. Hardly surprising when she'd told him that his services were no longer required. That he could go—not that he'd been intending to stay, she thought morosely.

Leading her into the main thoroughfare, he halted outside the hotel, nodded to the commissionaire who held the heavy glass door open for them, then led a now docile Davina to the bar, where he seated her at a secluded table. 'Excuse me for one moment. I just want to check on Ammy.' Searching her face, he asked, 'You will wait?'

She hesitated, then nodded.

'Order what you like from the waiter; I won't be long.'

A gin and tonic nursed in her palms, all the fight gone out of her, she stared at the opulent surroundings. One of the most expensive hotels in the city, and which he could easily afford. 'It would be best to talk about it', he'd said, and perhaps it was. Maybe he would be able to put it all into perspective. Maybe. Anyway, he was right about one thing: if she continued to behave like a frightened virgin, he might begin to suspect that there was a secret she needed to hide, and she most definitely didn't want that.

Needing a distraction, she glanced round her once more, noted the people at other tables. Not many, but all expensively dressed, especially the woman nearest to her. Jewels and furs, hardly needed on this warm evening. But if you had it you might as well flaunt it, she thought wryly. She watched the woman glance up, saw her eyes widen with interest, sit straighter in her seat, smile invitingly, and Davina knew, if she turned her head, whom she would see. Joel, who could captivate without even trying.

Looking down into her glass, she rattled the ice cubes, then gave a little grunt of laughter. She was being absurd, refusing to look at a man who was going to join her anyway. She could almost *feel* where he was in the room—close, a few yards away—and she finally looked up. Six feet of sex appeal, a creature of emotion, and she felt again that alarming little dip in her stomach, the accelerated beat of her heart, could recall the feeling, the taste of his tongue tracing her lips. Wrenching her mind away, she focused on what he was wearing. Ex-

quisitely tailored grey trousers fitted his long legs to perfection, the light blue shirt, cuffs rolled untidily back,
brightened his eyes. A gold watch was strapped to one
wrist, plain, understated, and probably worth a small
fortune, and the copy of her book was still in his hand,
picked up, presumably, in the hall where she had given
her talk. She hoped he'd paid for it.

Everyone in the bar was wearing a tie except Joel, and
no one, she knew, would tell him to go and put one on.
He was the sort of person you never told to do *anything*.
The elegant lift of one eyebrow was a whole vocabulary.

'Ammy all right?' she asked as he reached her, and
was annoyed to find that her voice was husky, disturbed.

He nodded, and if he noted the huskiness he didn't
let on, just looked away, and the waiter was already there,
hovering. With a faint smile that probably owed more
to despair than humour, she glanced at Diamonds-and-
furs, saw her chagrin, could almost hear her thoughts.
What's she got that I haven't? Davina was tempted to
tell her.

'Why the smile?' he asked softly as the waiter fussily
rearranged the white coaster and gently deposited the
glass of Scotch.

'Oh, nothing much.' Raising her glass, she silently
toasted him.

'To the past?' he asked. 'Memories?'

'No. The present.'

'Because that's safer?'

'Maybe.'

Picking up his glass, he took a long swallow, and then
flipped open her book at random.

'I hope you paid for it.'

'I did. Aloe vera,' he read. 'This remarkable suc-
culent may be planted in your garden, or, even better,

grown as a house plant as an anti-burn remedy and to alleviate the pain of insect bites.'

'It's also good for skin irritations and sunburn,' she put in tartly. 'And to soften rough skin.'

He glanced up, closed the book and leaned back, his glass now nursed in his palms, giving her a mocking smile. 'But I don't have rough skin, do I?' he asked softly.

'I don't remember,' she denied shortly. 'Only the rough tongue——' Cursing herself, she broke off. 'I didn't mean . . .'

'I know.' He looked hatefully amused.

'I meant . . .'

'I know. You have the plant in your kitchen, do you?'

'Yes.'

'Just grab a leaf and rub it on?'

'Break it open to release the juice, or gel, yes.'

'And you carry all these facts in your head?'

'Most of them.'

He looked faintly admiring. 'I don't know anything about you, do I?'

She shook her head.

'Tell me.'

Glancing at him, she asked, 'Why?'

'You know why.'

'No, Joel, I don't. Pursuit because I'm here? Because pursuit is as natural as breathing to you?'

'Is it?'

'So I understand.'

'You shouldn't believe all you read in the papers. Humour me. You look efficient, in control, a lady who knows where she's going.'

'Do I?' she asked stonily.

'Yes. Sensuality minimised.' And when her mouth tightened he gave a taunting smile as though he understood very well why she dressed as she did, everything tailored, businesslike. 'Power dressing, isn't that what they call it? Life on your terms. And it's all a lie, isn't it, Davina?' he asked negligently.

'Is it?'

'Yes. Afraid some other man might come along to pick the—fruit?' Leaning forward, as though to impart a confidence, he whispered softly, 'It doesn't work, Davina, only enhances the—temptation.' As though satisfied, he leaned back, deliberately sipped his drink. 'Tell me why you took up alternative medicine. I missed most of the talk.'

'What a pity. You might have learned something.'

'Don't be tart. Tell me.'

'My mother had arthritis,' she said shortly. And in a way her mother had been her saviour. She'd gone running home after the miscarriage, her tail between her legs, and had been horrified to find that her mother's illness wasn't just the nuisance she'd always insisted, but agonisingly debilitating, and she'd felt guilty for not knowing, understanding, for being wrapped up in her own concerns and forgetting her mother's. And so, in a desperate desire to banish the past, she had thrown all her energies into finding something that might help. Glancing at Joel, seeing that he was still patiently waiting, she sighed. 'Drugs controlled it, helped with the pain, but there is no real cure. The doctors didn't even really know what sort it was. There are so many different—varieties. And so I began reading up on the subject—libraries, herbalists.'

'And did you find something that helped?'

'Mmm. Ginger.'

'Ginger?' he asked in surprise. 'As in roast lamb?'

Deciding that she'd be a damn fool to give him any more weapons he might use, she forced herself to relax, gave a husky little laugh, nodded. 'Yes, as in roast lamb. It's easy to buy, sold in most supermarkets. A brilliant and under-used root. Grated and boiled for tea, baths—internal central heating. Gives a nice glow, and it helped with Mum's arthritis.'

'Cured it?'

'No-o, helped the pain, eased the symptoms. Burdock to detoxify...' With another wry smile, and perhaps because there was the width of a table between them, a small barrier to give the illusion of safety, she gave him a saucy old-fashioned look. 'Need detoxifying, do you?'

'Probably. If I knew what it meant. No, don't tell me, I can guess, and judging by the look you're giving my Scotch I assume that whisky does *not* get rid of toxins.'

'It might,' she smiled, 'if it made you sweat enough.'

'It doesn't. It either makes me maudlin—or amorous.'

'Joel...'

He grinned, not entirely companionably. 'How's your mother now?' he asked blandly.

'Not too bad. She and Dad moved to Florida. The damp and cold of England made her condition worse, so they went to live out there. Dad's into arthropods...'

'Arthropods?' he queried with a quirky smile.

'Insects, so he's more than happy with all the varieties to be found in the—um——'

'Everglades?'

'Yes. He writes books about them, which, thankfully, get published, so they can afford to stay.'

'A literary family.'

'Yes.'

'And we're skating all round the subject foremost in both our minds, aren't we?'

'Foremost in yours maybe, not foremost in mine.'

'Liar. Don't you want to know why I never got in touch with you?'

'I know why you didn't get in touch. You went back to your wife. Anyway——' she shrugged '—why should you? It was only a one-night——'

'Only? That was never "only", Davina. Never. I took your——'

'Don't,' she bit out, then forced herself to lightness. 'It had to go some——'

His hand shot out so fast that she didn't even see it. He grabbed her wrist, nearly making her spill her drink, forced her hand to the table. 'Don't,' he gritted, and for a moment he sounded almost savage. 'Don't you know that——?' Breaking off, he took a deep breath, released her, sat back. His mouth twisting, he said, 'I was being noble.'

'Noble?' she queried shakily.

'Yes.' Looking up, piercing her with his regard, he asked, 'Don't you think me capable of it?'

'I don't know,' she whispered.

'No, how should you?' Staring moodily down into his glass, he continued quietly, 'And that's not entirely true either. *Part* of me was being noble—after I'd rationalised your behaviour...'

'Rationalised?' she queried weakly. He *understood*?

'Yes, realised *why* you'd behaved as you had, but the other part blamed you for the temptation. And you were tempting, Davina. Still are.' Flicking his eyes up to hers, he asked flatly, 'How long did you eschew men for? Weeks? Months? Years?'

Shocked because he was so uncomfortably near the truth, she shook her head. 'It's none of——'

'My business,' he finished for her. 'No, it isn't.' With a sigh, his mood changing again, he added obscurely, 'A devil drives me sometimes. Dark, black... I do things, say things... Depraved.'

'No!' she exclaimed, shocked.

With a half-smile, he agreed, 'No, and it's a terrible thing, but that's how people *want* me to be. *Expect* me to be. Trundled out at parties, the devil incarnate. There's an excited buzz. How will he behave tonight? Smash things? Get drunk? Violent?'

'No!'

'No,' he agreed again, even more softly, 'but because I can be—cutting, because I once caused a scene at some dreadful party, I got a reputation. And that's what everyone wants, isn't it? Excitement, scandal. They *want* it to happen, expect it to—and say that it does. You wouldn't believe the things I've been accused of.'

'Womanising?'

'That too. It's *expected*.'

'And untrue?'

'Mostly. I wouldn't have *time* for all the affairs I'm reported to have.'

Meeting her concerned gaze, he gave her a curiously sweet smile. 'What did you expect of me that night, Vi—Davina?' he corrected absently. 'Divine one. Isn't that what it means?'

'Yes. And I didn't expect anything. Didn't *want* anything.'

'Except to punish me for Paul's perfidy?'

'Not you specifically...'

'No. I just happened to be there.'

'Yes,' she sighed. 'I wanted to expiate the pain, blame someone, hurt someone, be—better.'

'Yes. Be better. And I was well-known, wasn't I? Someone Paul might get to hear about.'

'Yes. No. Oh, Joel, I don't know. Subconsciously perhaps.' But it wasn't entirely that, she didn't think. It hadn't even been thought through. Just a reaction, an opportunity. He'd been strong, magnetic, and impossibly attractive. Arrogant and obviously experienced. Someone who would not read anything into their encounter. Someone who would not remind her of it afterwards, cause her embarrassment or grief. And that had to be the biggest joke of all time. 'And if you hadn't seen me last night...'

'Maybe, but I did see you last night.' Twisting his glass to and fro, throwing prisms of light from the overhead chandeliers, he added quietly, 'And wanted you.'

Ignoring the provocation, with difficulty, forcing back the warmth his words brought, she stated, 'Because it was unfinished business?'

'Perhaps,' he agreed. 'And perhaps because you're beautiful, because you're a woman most men would want to—hold.'

It wasn't said admiringly, or yearningly, but as a statement of fact.

'And you're a man who likes women.'

He smiled faintly, gave an infuriating shrug.

'And Ammy's falling asleep today was just an excuse.'

'Yes,' he admitted. 'A *raison d'être*.' Leaning back, he stared at her. 'How did you sleep last night?' he asked softly.

Looking quickly down, she refused to answer.

'As badly as I did? I kept remembering... No, that's not strictly true; I remembered it all in very vivid detail the moment I saw you walk into the party last night. Not that I'd ever really forgotten,' he added almost jeeringly. 'You're a very beautiful woman, sexy—and I wanted to feel the same response that I felt all those years ago. Does that disgust you?'

She mutely shook her head, because hadn't she, even briefly, wanted that too? 'But it won't happen, Joel. Too much water has passed under the bridge.' Before he could pursue it, if that was his intention, she quickly finished her drink and got to her feet. He didn't look entirely surprised.

'I'll walk you back.'

'No—it's not far, only a few yards. And anyway, Ammy might wake,' she added with divine inspiration.

Reaching the foyer, she stupidly held out her hand. He looked at it, then at her, and she let it drop to her side. Turning away, she gave the doorman an automatic smile as he opened the door for her, heard Joel murmur something to him, saw from the corner of her eye a note change hands, and then he was beside her. He caught her hand in his, tangled his fingers with hers, and said softly, 'Remember?'

She gave a jerky nod, tried to free her hand as she so very vividly recalled how it had all begun. How he had tangled his fingers in hers, drawn her against him.

'A smoky room,' he murmured, 'noisy, everyone else having fun. Except you—and me. We stood at opposite ends of the room, both leaning against a wall...'

And every time the revellers had shifted his gaze would be on her—and hers on his. And then he'd left the room, and she'd followed. He hadn't looked surprised to find her behind him, had merely turned, given her a twisted smile, and reached for her hand. Heat flooding through her, she tried to wrench her mind away, and skipped to

later, when he'd insisted on taking her home. The no[
and the warmth of the party left behind, she'd shivere[
Fear? A realisation of what she had done? Or simply
because she'd been cold? He hadn't spoken, merely
linked his fingers round her cold hand, pushed them both
into his coat pocket.

'Only a few weeks into the new year,' she whispered
now, not wanting to remember, but somehow com-
pelled. 'A cold, crisp January night.'

'Yes. The night you should have begun your
honeymoon. A day that should have been your wedding-
day.'

'Yes.' Had she told him that? She couldn't remember,
only that bitter anger, that desire for retribution had returned. There'd been a ring around the moon, she remembered, and in the shadow of the Hammersmith
flyover they'd leaned on the river wall, stared down into
the water. Her mind had been on Paul, wishing almost
savagely that he could somehow know what he had for-
feited, know what she had just given this man, this
stranger—a man different from any other she'd ever met.
Commanding, distant-looking, arrogant, as though he
shaped the world to his liking, not the other way about,
slightly dissolute, an air of unutterable boredom that had
covered a simmering anger. She'd gone with him out of
a deep hurt, defiance—and for over four years had been
trying to banish it from her mind. And if he stayed in
her life, however briefly, he would be a constant reminder of things she wanted to forget. A reminder of
the person she had once been, and was no longer.

'We walked for miles, didn't we? Along dark, silent
streets, the only people in the world, or so it seemed,
and then we reached your flat, and you invited me inside,
to make love again, this time in comfort.' His voice cool,

without inflexion, as though he were relating something
of no interest, he continued, 'And later that morning,
when you woke, you told me to go. Told me I was a
substitute.'

'Yes,' she admitted, 'because I realised what I had
done, knew you must think me cheap.' Halting, she
looked up at him, still ashamed of her behaviour. Not
only because she had used him, however willing he might
have been, but because she had told him so.

'When do you leave?' he asked abruptly.

She gave a little start, that old memory so vivid, so
real, her mouth half-open to tender a belated apology,
relieve her guilt, and it took her a moment to realise that
this was a different time, that they had stopped in front
of the courtyard to her apartment. 'What? Oh, in the
morning.' Searching his eyes, perhaps trying to see if he
truly did understand, and seeing only the look he had
given her on waking all those years ago, she swallowed
hard, looked quickly away.

'And if I asked for your home address,' he asked dis-
tantly, 'would you give it me?'

'No,' she whispered, and it seemed for a moment as
though it was the hardest thing she had ever done. But
once had been foolish. Perhaps understandable, but
foolish. Twice would be—disastrous. And she didn't
think he *really* wanted it.

'So this is goodbye?'

'Yes,' she agreed on a soft breath, and was then taken
completely by surprise when he reached out, drew her
against him, held her against his length.

Dragging in a deep breath, alarmed at the way her
body felt just touching his, she protested huskily, 'People
will see.' She didn't know if they could, but it felt as
though they might, as though curtains were twitching.

'Let them see,' he said arrogantly.

'Let me go,' she pleaded.

He did the opposite. The arm round her tightened imperceptibly and with his free hand he grasped her hair, gently tugged so that she was forced to look up... not far—in her heels she wasn't that much shorter than he— but it brought his mouth on a level with her own.

'No,' she whispered against his mouth.

'You're trembling.'

'No.'

He said something she didn't hear, touched his mouth to hers, and as though it were yesterday, a yesterday of over four years ago, like a magnet, it clung. Releasing her hair, he smoothed his palm down her back, a movement that was almost urgent, and the heat of his hand as it pressed briefly against her spine was nearly her undoing. And then he moved to caress her lower back beneath her jacket, press her against him, and she gasped.

Heat seemed to be coming off him in waves, exciting her, melting her, and for one long moment she forgot where they were, forgot the curious gazes they might be attracting from apartments or passers-by, and for all her protests of denial she leaned into him, revelling in sensations she had not felt for a very long time.

He dragged a breath deep into his lungs, moved fractionally away, stared at her, and in the light from the overhead lamp his beautiful eyes were a deep, deep blue, the pupils wide, enlarged, mesmerising. 'Don't look at me like that,' he reproved. He sounded almost angry.

'Like what? I'm not looking at you like anything.'

'Yes, you are. With anxiety, a plea in those lovely eyes not to hurt you. The way you looked at me all those years ago.'

'No...'

'What's his name?' he demanded abruptly.

'What?' she asked dazedly.

'The boyfriend.'

'Michael,' she fabricated quickly.

'Another substitute?'

It took her a moment to realise what he meant. 'No!' she denied. 'No.'

'Then I hope you get what you deserve.' With a curt nod, he turned, and she watched him walk away, listened to the echo of his quick footsteps along the pavement. Feeling shaken, almost distraught, she swallowed hard, pushed blindly through the gate and hurried across to her front door. Deserve? For good, she wondered, or ill? The inflexion had been—derisive. *Had* he been mocking her? Paying her back? The things he'd said, the feelings he'd hinted at, all a lie? His pride had been hurt—and this was punishment?

CHAPTER THREE

SLEEP didn't come easily, for the second night. Davina's body yearned for a closeness that she kept denying it. A deep ache, like an itch, that wouldn't go away, and when exhaustion finally did claim her her dreams were haunted by a dark-haired man—she was being chased, hunted—and when she was caught he was laughing. A joke, he would say, just a joke. And in her dreams she cried.

When she woke the next morning it was late, her plan to be away early thwarted, but not her determination for immunity, to steer well clear of Joel Gilman in future— and she tried desperately to clear the depression that that determination brought. Tried to hate him for his mockery. Tried to understand that it was—expected, and just felt used. As he had once felt?

By the time she'd tidied the apartment, had something to eat, loaded up her car, posted the apartment key back through the letterbox, it was after eleven—and then she discovered that the Envalira Pass was temporarily closed, which accounted for the heavy and often stationary traffic clogging the narrow road. Wanting to cry, feeling disgruntled and out of sorts, as though fate were conspiring against her, she locked the car, and decided to have a wander round the small town. Fight it, she told herself grimly. Just keep fighting it.

Her bag slung over one shoulder, hands shoved into her jean pockets, she joined the hundreds of other people doing the same thing. The shopkeepers, who all seemed to be doing a roaring trade, were no doubt delighted, and with a faintly bitter smile she wondered if *that* was a conspiracy. Takings in the shops were down, so they closed the pass. Tourists got bored, were at a loose end, so went shopping to pass the time. Trade went up, the pass was opened, and everyone was happy.

There was scaffolding on lots of the buildings, getting ready for the summer season, perhaps, repairing the ravages caused by the winter's heavy snowfalls, and as she edged round a knot of people arguing the merit or otherwise of driving back into Spain and so circumnavigating the closed pass she saw Joel. Halting, she just stared at him, her eyes bleak. He was dressed in black— black jeans, black polo shirt—Ammy held carefully by one hand. The devil incarnate. No, that wasn't true, but still someone to be avoided. Someone who could hurt her—someone who was already hurting her. She had wished, foolishly, in the night that she were the sort of person who could take life as it came, meet the good and the bad head-on and damn the consequences, but she *couldn't* be like that; she could only be herself, cope with life as best she could. She'd been hurt very badly once, and hurt again by Joel, because emotion had taken over; not strictly his fault, she supposed, and perhaps, in all honesty, it was easier to blame him than herself for her stupidity, but she knew she couldn't cope with being hurt again. And he would hurt her, if she let him. Cowardly maybe, to run away, but that was the way she was. It was easy for other people to say, Take a chance, but not all other people bore the scars she did. Or maybe it wasn't the scars; maybe she was just too sensitive.

Dodging beneath the scaffolding, she turned to walk back the way she had come. She heard the shout from above her, but it didn't really register because her mind was still fixed on Joel, and so she was taken completely by surprise when she was roughly grasped and dragged out into the road.

'Hey...' she began, and then gasped when a pile of bricks crashed to the pavement at the exact spot where she'd been standing.

'Don't you have any more sense than to walk under scaffolding when workmen are using it?' Joel demanded furiously.

Staring at him with shocked eyes, she couldn't answer, and then only slowly registered the fact that an angry graze ran from his forehead to his cheekbone, narrowly missing his eye. It was painted yellow, of all things, with some kind of embrocation. 'Is that what you did?' she asked shakily.

'What?'

Reaching out a trembling hand, she stopped short of actually touching the angry wound.

'No,' he denied impatiently.

'Then how did you do it?'

'I walked into a door,' he said shortly. 'For God's sake, Davina! You could have been killed!'

'Yes,' she whispered, and dragged a deep breath into her lungs in an effort to steady herself. 'Thank you.'

He gave a soft curse under his breath and steered her across the road and into a café. Pushing her none too gently into a seat, he lifted Ammy to sit beside her, then walked across to the counter.

Managing a smile for the little girl, who was staring at her with wide eyes, she moved her gaze to Joel. *He* didn't have to squeeze through the crush: people parted like the Red Sea. He didn't hover impatiently waiting to be served, but commanded instant attention, *expected* instant attention. He looked aloof, arrogant as he attracted the barman's attention, and she saw people turn to look at him, as though he was someone important, special. Which he was, she supposed drearily. He also had very quick reflexes. If he hadn't, she... And only then did her mind finally catch up with the fact that she could have been killed. Clenching her hands tight on the table, she forced herself to concentrate on something else, anything else, and watched Joel turn, walk back towards them, a waiter hurrying at his heels balancing a tray of coffee and brandy.

'Drink it,' he ordered, passing her one of the tiny balloon glasses.

'I don't li——'

'Drink it!'

Davina drank, then choked. Glaring at him, wiping the tears from her eyes, she put the glass down and reached for her coffee. 'You don't have to shout at me.'

'Someone needs to!' Sitting opposite her, waving the waiter away with an impatient hand, he drank his own brandy in one swallow. 'You don't have the brains of a rocking-horse,' he continued to castigate angrily. 'Didn't you hear the workman shout?'

'Yes. No.' Raking her hair back with a hand that still shook, she focused on anything rather than him. 'I'm all right,' she assured him shakily. She had to cope with this, with him, pretend his mockery of the night before didn't matter. When he didn't answer, she glanced round. Blue eyes were regarding her broodingly, and she hastily looked down, stared at the front of his shirt. Red brick dust clung to the black material, and one shoulder was hunched awkwardly. 'Did you hurt your shoulder?' she asked stiffly, still without raising her eyes to his.

'I dislocated it,' he said shortly.

'Just now?' she exclaimed, shocked. 'Then you have
to——'

'Earlier,' he interrupted brusquely.

'Earlier?' She frowned.

'Yes.' With an impatient sigh he reached for his coffee,
and she heard him swallow, caught the movement in his
throat, and found that she had an absurd desire to burst
into tears. Raising her eyes to his, forcing emotion aside,
she asked, 'How?'

'Door,' Ammy said.

Moving her eyes to the little girl, who was regarding
her with an odd mixture of fascination and worry, she
queried gently, 'Door?'

'Man did it.'

Switching her gaze back to Joel, she waited, and he
gave an irritable twitch, explaining, 'Some lunatic let
the heavy glass hotel door go on an elderly woman. I
lunged to catch it and dislocated my shoulder. All right?'
he asked with heavy sarcasm.

'Where was the doorman?' she demanded, as though
it actually mattered.

'How should I know?'

'And your face?'

'The eagle.'

'Eagle?' she asked in bewilderment.

'Big,' Ammy offered.

An absurd vision of an eagle swooping to attack him
made her blink, then smile and instantly deny the image.
'Eagle?' she repeated, and then realised, recalled the large
stone griffins that stood either side of the hotel entrance, and nodded her understanding. 'The heavy door
pulled you off balance and you scraped your face on the
statue?' He gave a derisive little inclination of his head.
'You've been to the hospital?'

The movement was repeated, even more derisively.

Frowning at him, she asked worriedly, 'But didn't they give you a sling?'

'Took it off,' Ammy volunteered proudly.

'Snitch,' he muttered as he gave his daughter a comical underbrow glance. She giggled.

'But Joel...'

'Don't fuss,' he bit out tersely. 'It's perfectly all right.'

'It is not perfectly all right!'

'Soon be better,' Ammy piped up, with her funny little nod, and Joel turned to her again, smiled.

'Soon be better,' he agreed, and his voice was gentle, a marked contrast to the tone he'd been using on Davina.

'Don't cry,' she added with that comical little shake of her head.

'No, I won't cry.' But Davina wanted to, and had to sniff, swallow hard.

Joel glanced up, looked astonished. 'What are you grizzling for?'

'I'm not grizzling,' she denied crossly. 'What did the doctor say?'

'That I was lucky,' he said drily.

'And to wear the sling?'

Leaning towards her, he said succinctly, 'I am not walking around in a bl——' Glancing quickly at his daughter, he substituted crossly, 'Sling!'

'You'd rather lose the use of your arm? Don't be so irresponsible! If you didn't need it, they wouldn't have given it to you!'

He ignored her. 'Finish your coffee.'

With a cross little tut, she did so. 'I suppose you'll just have to hope that when you're ready to leave it will be well enough to enable you to drive. Unless you came by chauffeur-driven limousine.'

'I didn't, and I'm leaving today.'

'Don't be absurd! You can't drive with a dislocated shoulder... Oh, no,' she denied hastily. '*I'm* not driving you out of Andorra.'

'Did I ask you to?'

'No, the look said it for you!'

He gave a slow smile that wasn't in the least friendly. 'Let's go and get some lunch.' Tossing a few coins on to the table, he got to his feet, helped Ammy down, and waited.

Her mouth tight, Davina got angrily to her feet, grabbed up her bag and, head high, preceded them out and into the street.

Halting her, he said quietly, 'It's this way.'

Her back to him, she denied, 'No, it isn't. I'm going back to my car.'

'It could be hours before the pass is open, in which case we'll have lunch. Stop cutting off your nose to spite your face. Anyway,' he added with that quirk of humour that always took her by surprise, 'you owe me. I just saved your life.'

Swinging round, she opened her mouth, then closed it again. He looked—grey, and that was the *only* reason, she assured herself, why she would accompany him along to the hotel. Because he looked—ill.

'Put a brave face on it, Davina,' he said softly as the now restored doorman held the door open to allow them all inside. 'Michael would be proud of you.'

'Shut up—and don't push your luck, Gilman.' And if Michael had actually existed, or actually existed as a lover, he wouldn't have been proud of her at all; he'd have told her she was a sentimental fool. He would also have been jealous. If she'd been engaged to him, which she wasn't. 'Anyway,' she added loftily, 'I do things because *I* want to, not because of anyone else. I make my own decisions.'

'Of course you do,' he agreed. 'The dining-room's this way.'

Trailing after him, she demanded, 'Is your car an automatic?'

'It is.'

'Well, then, you could probably drive it. What did the doctor say?'

'She didn't.'

'Because you didn't ask?'

'Correct.' Halting, he glanced at her over his shoulder. 'Road is the only way out of Andorra,' he told her softly, as though she didn't know, 'and the car, naturally, is a right-hand drive. I can't wait for my shoulder to heal. I have to get back to England within the next few days. Have to get Ammy back to her mother.'

Her mouth still tight, she followed him into the dining-room, watched the concern of the *maître d'* as he hurried across to them, gave a slightly cynical smile at the deference he was shown.

Joel ordered paella for them all, without consultation, merely raising one eyebrow at Davina, and she gave in and nodded. Not that any of them was very hungry, and they hardly did justice to the meal, just picked at it, and, no matter how many times she told herself she wasn't going to drive him, all the arguments she put forward to herself sounded petty, spiteful. 'You could hire a driver.'

'I could.' Raising his eyes from his plate, he watched her, waited.

'Or you could leave your car here, get a cab or something to the nearest airpor——'

'No.'

Startled, she queried, 'No?'

He shook his head. 'I don't fly.'

'Don't? What, never?'

'No.'

The expression in his eyes warned her not to ask why. 'You want someone to drive you all the way back?'

'I don't *want* anything—that someone isn't prepared to give,' he tacked on softly.

Looking quickly away, she rearranged her meal on her plate, idly making concentric patterns. And if she kept refusing, he would wonder why, wouldn't he? 'You could get a train. From France, I mean.'

'I could,' he agreed quietly.

Throwing down her fork, she snapped shortly, 'All right! I'll drive you!'

'Thank you. If it were just myself, I'd make the attempt, but with Ammy in the car...'

'I've said,' she gritted, 'I'll do it!'

He nodded, and if just one triumphant smile crossed his lips, just a tiny hint of one, she would retract, she promised herself grimly. He didn't smile.

'We could do a stop-over in France somewhere,' he murmured smoothly, 'and it should be easy enough to get a ferry this early in the seas——'

'To the station!'

'Ah.' His smile curled. 'It's still a long way...'

'I *know* it's a long way!' But not as far as to the ferry, and if they stopped, as they would probably need to, that would make two days of his company instead of one. It would be bad enough having his disruptive presence in the car beside her for the couple of hours it would take to get to the nearest station; further enforced intimacies she was not prepared to accept. 'Station,' she repeated.

He nodded, looked as though his tongue was stuck in his cheek, and she silently dared him to comment. Anyway, a few hours wasn't so much. She could cope with that, couldn't she? Suddenly remembering that kiss, the way he'd made her feel, she wasn't so sure, but she was perfectly capable of keeping him at a distance—she'd been doing it to men for years, and she couldn't leave him stranded, could she? Not when he'd saved her from a nasty injury, possibly death. Couldn't allow him to drive with Ammy in the car... You don't have to make excuses to *yourself*, she told herself crossly, then said, 'I'll go and ring the hire-car company, tell them to pick my car up from here. Go and collect my luggage...'

'The porter will do it.'

Yes, and therein lay the difference between them. He paid minions to do things for him, she did things herself. With a little shrug, she gave in.

Looking down at his daughter, at her uneaten meal, he asked gently, 'Don't want any more, Moppet?'

She shook her head. 'All finished.'

'Want anything else? Pudding? Ice-cream?'

'No,' she replied. 'Ammy get down.'

'All right. Davina?'

'No, I don't seem to be very hungry either.' Rescuing her fork, she laid it tidily on her plate.

'We'll have coffee in the lounge.' Calling over the waiter, he settled the bill, asked to have their coffee taken through to the comfortable seating area just beyond the dining-room, helped his daughter down, and led the way out.

'I'll go and ring the hire company.'

He nodded, settled himself on a long sofa, Ammy cuddled beside him, and Davina walked to the bank of nearby telephones.

When she returned, a porter was waiting for her car keys so that he could retrieve her luggage, and she handed them over, sat in the armchair facing Joel and his daughter, and reached forward to pour her own coffee.

'The pass is open,' he informed her quietly.

She nodded to show she'd heard, then gave him a critical glance. He looked terrible, his head resting back, eyes half closed, watching her between his lashes, and then he gave an odd, slightly wry smile.

'Not how I intended it.'

'No.' Intended what? she wondered. Their meeting? Their parting? Or merely his trip out to Andorra? 'How do you feel?'

'Rough.'

'Yes, I imagine you do, and I really do think that——'

'Don't,' he reproved softly, 'tell me that I need to lie down, need to put the sling on. I just want to get out of here, go home.'

Yes, she thought with a sigh, going home was always best.

When the porter returned with her keys, he smiled at her and, his English stilted, formal, he asked politely, 'You would permit me to hold on to them? Return them to whoever collects your car?'

'Oh, yes, please, that would be kind.'

He gave a gracious little nod, turned his attention to Joel, handed him his own car keys. 'I've put madam's case in your car, sir, brought it round to the front. I'm sorry this should have happened in our country, and I hope you will soon be fully recovered. Have a safe journey home.'

'Yes, thanks.' His smile slightly cynical, Joel reached into his pocket, tipped him generously, helped Ammy down, and got to his feet. 'Let's go.'

Quickly finishing her coffee, Davina stood, slung her bag over her shoulder, gave the porter another warm smile and followed Joel and his daughter out of the hotel.

'No need to gush, Davina,' Joel observed drily.

'Because you paid him handsomely to serve? Because you knew that's why he did it? It makes no difference. Politeness costs nothing.'

'No,' he agreed. Halting, he gave her an odd smile. 'No,' he repeated, 'it doesn't. I think I've been around the wrong people too long. Can you . . . ?' he began, and Davina nodded, smiled at Ammy, helped her into her child seat in the back of the car and strapped her safely in, then walked round to the driver's door while Joel climbed into the passenger seat, fastened his seatbelt, leaned back and closed his eyes.

The wrong people? People with money who expected, and paid for, the best? Whose manners tended to slip? But Joel wasn't like that. How do you know, Davina? He might very well be like that, she told herself. With a sigh, she pulled out into the slow-moving traffic and, once clear of the town, finally managed to pick up speed. The car was easy to drive, comfortable, expensive, top of the range, and the engine didn't so much growl as purr menacingly. Feeling somewhat tired herself after the drama of the morning, keeping her mind very firmly away from the man who sat beside her, she drove carefully until used to the vehicle, then slowly relaxed, grateful for a silent Joel, a silent Ammy in the back seat. She pushed away the niggling thought that she was exactly where she wanted to be.

Snow clung to the tops of the mountains, like icing on a cake, hid in shadowed ravines where the sun could not reach, and as she climbed higher the air turned cooler, the sky above a perfect blue. Soon summer would carpet the fleetingly glimpsed meadows with flowers, warm those rugged slopes. Ski chalets would be shut up until the season began again, or maybe leased to summer visitors. Misty clouds hovered at the edge of each drop as though trying to find a firmer footing, grasp the edge of the road, and as the traffic slowed towards the head of the pass she glanced at her passenger, found him watching her, stared briefly into blue eyes that put the sky to shame, into a strong face, a face she had touched, a mouth she had kissed, and she shivered.

'Cold?'

She shook her head, then jumped in alarm when he reached out, touched a strand of her hair that had blown across her mouth, and gently removed it. 'I'm glad,' he said softly.

'Glad?' she whispered thickly. 'That I'm not cold?'

'No, that we met again. That it didn't—end.'

'But it has ended,' she blurted quickly. 'You made that very clear last night. This is just...'

'Yes,' he agreed, 'this is just—the finale.'

'You paid me back, and——'

'Your own objections were duly noted,' he agreed drily. 'I've never forced my attentions on a woman, and I don't intend to start now.'

Had never needed to, she thought dully, and now didn't want to.

'You are driving me into France, for which I am very grateful.'

'And that's all,' she insisted, with a rather hollow ache inside.

'Yes, Davina, that's all.'

'Good.' And that was where she should have left it—but found herself unable to. 'It *was* just a game, wasn't it? To pay me back.'

'No.'

'What, then? A challenge? Out of boredom?'

'Possibly. Tell me about your tour,' he instructed as he eased himself into a slightly more comfortable position. 'Where you've been, what you've done. You said you were in northern Spain.'

'Yes.' 'Possibly'? Not said tentatively, or reflectively, but flatly. But if it hadn't been that, what else could it have been? Brief, she told herself, trying for humour, and galling, that he hadn't deemed her worth a lengthy chase, or even a very determined one, which was irrational, because she didn't want him to chase her. Really she didn't. Or had he been disappointed in her? Found her vastly changed from that young Davina...

'Spain?' he prompted.

'What? Oh, yes, Spain. I talked herbal talk with people,' she began somewhat absently as her mind continued, against her will, to try and find a reason for his behaviour, 'exchanged ideas, saw the sights, cathedrals and monasteries, the Picos de Europa.'

'I thought they were all mountains,' he frowned. 'Can you drive through them?'

'The river valleys, yes, and where there are no roads you can walk.'

'Looking for herbs?'

'Yes, of course. What else would I be looking for? It's my life. What I do.'

'*Only* what you do?' he asked with a provoking little smile.

'Yes. No! Oh, shut up, Joel. I worked hard to get where I am, achieve what I've achieved...'

'Did I say different?'

'No, but I'm actually quite proud of myself.'

'You have every reason to be.'

'Yes.' Yet somewhere along the way she'd missed out on—life. Pushing the thought aside, she allowed the car to creep forward. It was nearly their turn to enter the pass, and she felt a slight frisson of nerves, remembered hair-raising tales about its steepness. Forcing herself to think about something else, she answered Joel more fully. 'I wanted to see where the herbs grew—see a wild horse perhaps. I didn't have time to see much because I missed the early bus.'

'Bus?' he queried, a little flicker of amusement in his eyes.

'Yes, I thought it would be easier than taking the car. It runs to the village of Posada de Valdeon.'

'Ah—and there's no need to sound so defensive. I really am interested.'

'Are you?' she asked sceptically as she nosed on to the pass. Mist swirled, ragged and insubstantial, then parted to show her the way. Sturdy railings guarded the drop; moisture clung to the rock beside her.

'Yes. So did you see it all?'

'What? Oh, no, a day isn't nearly long enough to see everything,' she murmured as she forced herself to concentrate on the unwinding spiral.

'Such as wild horses?'

'Yes. Take the cable car from Fuente Dé into a wilderness of shattered limestone,' she explained, gripping the wheel too hard until her fingers cramped in protest. 'The palaeolithic paintings in the caves at Buxu. I did manage to see the monastery... Ah,' she gasped as the turn was tighter than she anticipated, and she fought not to snatch at the wheel, over-correct.

'Go on,' he said soothingly, gently, 'you're doing fine.'

She gave a shaky laugh. 'I don't feel fine, I feel like a rank novice! What a spiral!'

'Yes.'

'And this mist keeps obscuring my vision!'

'Just watch the car in front's brake lights and you'll be fine. What about the monastery?'

'Hmm? Oh, at Covadonga, where the legendary King Pelayo fended off the Moors in—oh, AD seven hundred and something or other.'

'That's good.'

Oblivious to his teasing, aware only of the need to keep her attention on what she was doing, she continued almost inaudibly, 'But I didn't have time to go on and see the glacial lakes.'

'Pity; I believe they're well worth seeing.'

Startled, she finally registered his amusement, which she found quite extraordinary in the circumstances, because she had assumed he was a man who always liked to be in control. Certainly not someone to crack weak jokes while being driven down a hair-raising pass by a woman rigid with nerves. Although had she been driving her own car, alone, she didn't think she would have been half so apprehensive. Diverted, she gave a weak snort of laughter. 'You've never even heard of them, have you?'

'No, but you make a very good talking guidebook. Are there really wild horses?'

'Mm, and griffon vultures, peregrine falcons, eagles, wild boar...'

'See them all, did you?'

She smiled again, shook her head. 'Only the chamois, but oh, Joel, it's so beautiful there, with the magnificent beechwoods, the—— My God, did you see that?' she exclaimed. 'That piece of railing was actually broken! Someone must have...'

'Not necessarily,' he soothed. 'It could have been caused by snow, a rock-fall. So, you intend to go back one day? See it all properly?'

'Yes, wander the mule tracks carved from the walls of the gorge, cross fragile bridges slung high above thundering rivers, explore the hay meadows, see the wild jasmine and barberry, strawberry and turpentine trees.'

'Now turpentine trees I *might* be interested in. What do you say, Moppet?' When there was no answer, he turned in his seat, glanced back, then smiled. 'She's asleep. Best thing for shock.'

'Yes,' she agreed drily, and flicked him a reproving glance.

He gave her a droll look. 'I'm not the only one who was shocked—and if we could have slept *together*...'

'Very funny,' she muttered, but it didn't stop the little frisson of alarm that ran through her. At least, she told herself it was alarm. 'And there's no need to pretend...'

'Admiration?'

'Yes! This is *me* remember?'

'Mmm. Not much further,' he added blandly. 'It's a more or less straight road after this.'

'Good,' she said fervently. 'And how you ever thought you would manage with a dislocated shoulder I don't know!'

'It isn't dislocated. The doctor put it back—and I wasn't intending to manage,' he added quietly.

'What?'

'Keep your eyes on the road!'

Wrenching her gaze back, she waited for her heart-rate to settle before asking shakily, 'What do you mean, you weren't intending to? If you hadn't met me——'

'Davina,' he broke in softly, 'I didn't see you by *accident* this morning.'

'Of course you did! I was behind you!'

He smiled. 'You can trail people from in front just as easily as from behind, you know, especially when there are large plate-glass windows of shops to facilitate it.'

'You were *watching* me?'

'Mmm.'

'But why?'

'You know why.'

Yes. 'Because you'd dislocated your damned shoulder and needed a driver!' She was disgusted with herself, although heaven knew why she should be, because she had *known* he always had an eye to the main chance.

'Disappointed?' he taunted.

'No. Why did you and Celia split up?' she asked bluntly. 'You keep asking about me, but you've been pretty close-mouthed about your own life.'

'I didn't think you'd be interested.'

'I'm not! It will pass the time,' she tacked on lamely.

'So it will.'

Throwing him a suspicious glance, but seeing nothing in his face to alarm her, she insisted, 'Well?'

'A combination of things. Claustrophobia, irritation, anger—incompatibility.'

'On both sides?'

'Mmm.'

'And that's it?'

'Yes. History.'

And they said a clam was close-mouthed!

'But what I'd dearly love to know,' he added softly, 'is how you knew we'd got back together in the first place.'

Startled, because it had never occurred to her that he might wonder *how* she had known, staring wide-eyed through the windscreen, she burbled, 'Because... because someone told me!'

'Who?' he asked in the same oh, so soft voice.

'Well, I don't know, do I? It was a long time ago!' She certainly had no intention of telling him that she'd gone *looking* for him, asked about him, found out he still had a *wife*! Flicking him a glance, to find that he was watching her, amusement lurking in his blue eyes, she snapped her head back to the front. Fool, Davina, why the hell didn't you make someone up? she castigated herself. The woman who'd held that party, perhaps... 'Why wasn't your mother maternal?' she demanded in an effort to distract him.

'If you can't answer, change the subject?' he asked in obvious amusement. 'Good defensive tactics, and how the hell should I know why she wasn't maternal? Presumably because she didn't like children. I probably take after her.'

'You like children,' she pointed out. 'You have Ammy.'

'Yes, the one commitment I value above all others.'

'You don't *have* any other commitments,' she scoffed.

'Don't I?'

'No.'

'How do you know? I might have a lot of little Ammys running around for all you know.'

Her heart jerked, steadied, and then she gave a grim smile. '*Do* you?'

'No,' he denied softly.

'Nor want any?'

'No.'

'Ever?'

'Does it matter?'

No, because she was probing an old wound that shouldn't be probed.

'I don't think I even ever wanted to marry,' he added more honestly. 'I like my independence.'

'And the dare-devilry I read about from time to time? What's that? A death-wish?'

'Good heavens, no! And I'd hardly call hang-gliding, or even saloon-car racing, *dare*-devilry. Fun, yes. Relaxation. What on earth made you think I might have a death-wish?'

'I don't know,' she shrugged. 'Because your mother wasn't maternal? Because you seem incapable of sustaining a relationship?'

He looked astonished. As well he might, she thought, furious with herself for even trying to understand him. 'You should stick to herbs,' he advised. 'Psychology obviously leaves you confused, and you really shouldn't believe all the gossip you hear, because that's mostly all it is—gossip. I had one serious relationship, with Celia— does the fact that we split up make me a death-defying monster?'

'No.' *One* serious relationship? Did that then reduce hers with him to—what? An experiment? An aberration?

'Painting is a static occupation... standing for hours, concentration, eye-strain, mind clouded with colour— my dare-devilry, as you call it, is merely escapism. A way to stretch cramped muscles, give my mind something else to think about.'

'Buy yourself a bike,' she muttered.

'Hardly a challenge.'

'And is that what I was? A challenge?'

He didn't answer, merely reproved, 'And before you commiserate with me on having had a wretched childhood because my mother wasn't maternal, don't, because it wasn't.'

Wasn't it? Not an emotional void he was unable now to fill? And why on earth did it matter to her so much? Why this need to excuse behaviour she knew nothing about? As he had said, best stick to herbs. They might affect the senses, but they didn't damage the heart.

'What was *your* childhood like?' he asked mockingly.

'Terrific.'

'Good. And now I think I'll take your advice and sleep for a bit. You'll be all right?'

'Yes,' she agreed, but she wasn't. She wasn't all right at all.

'No need to look so worried,' he mocked. 'Wake me if there's a problem.'

'And what will you do?' she enquired tartly. 'Fend off dragons?'

'With my good right arm,' he promised. Wriggling into a more comfortable position, he closed his eyes.

With a little snort, she stared grimly through the windscreen. Thought he was an expert on women, did he? Knew how they felt, thought? Well, not *this* woman. 'I think you have to be the most...' Catching herself up, she bit her lip. It was so easy to fall into argument with him, but that wasn't the way to keep him at a distance, and she *needed* to do that. She didn't want a relationship with him—well, he didn't want one with her; he'd said so.

You're chagrined.

No, I'm not!

Yes, you are; you *wanted* him to pursue you!

Didn't.

Did.

Only for the satisfaction of slapping him down.

Liar.

Oh, for the love of Pete, Davina, will you just shut up?

With a disgruntled sigh she glanced at him, at the innate strength in that face, the arrogant certainty that he was always right, then returned her troubled gaze to the road. What would have happened if...? Wrenching her mind violently away, she glanced at Ammy through the rear-view mirror, saw that she was still sleeping, and allowed her mind to wander once more. For over four years she'd been Miss Don't Touch, Miss Efficient, stood on her own two feet, emotions concealed. Now here was Joel, who had known her before those same emotions could be imprisoned, and she was behaving like the person she'd once been. In other words, a little voice whispered mockingly, she was being herself, and she had to admit that it felt good... not needing to watch her words—well, only certain words—in case she gave a man the wrong impression. Joel, unbelievable as it was, seemed to *understand* her. She'd had four years without a relationship, four years of being cool, businesslike, keeping the men she dated at a distance. And Michael, who was *not* her fiancé but her editor, who did not love her, whom she did not love in return, treated her as she treated him—with respect. They had lunch together, dined, met in his office, but it was a businesslike relationship. As all her relationships were. And now, thanks to Joel, and Ammy, she admitted honestly, a crack had appeared in her armour; emotion was leaking through. Seal up the cracks, Davina, she thought with a sigh. Seal them up. You've avoided relationships this far because you didn't want to be hurt again, and allowing Joel in, even on the lightest level, would not only hurt, but destroy.

Unable to keep her eyes off him, she flicked him another glance. He was so very attractive, confident, and the contrast between his dark hair, lashes and pale skin was devastating. She tried to convince herself that she had only offered to drive him out of compassion, but it wasn't true, and she suspected he knew it wasn't true; but for her own sanity she *must* revert to the person she'd been before Joel had erupted into her life again. She must put the casing back, only she had a horrible feeling that the casing was warped, exposing gaping holes where the seams had been. And are you intending to spend the rest of your life avoiding emotional involvement, Davina? In case you should get hurt again? she asked herself. Not knowing the answer, she returned her attention to her driving—not easy when Joel continued to twitch and murmur beside her, his sleep far from peaceful. But then she doubted that this man was ever peaceful, even when he was in a good mood.

As though somehow aware of her thoughts, he sighed, turned his face the other way, then hissed and abruptly woke as the damaged side of his face came into contact with the seat. He straightened, blinked, snapped his head round as though surprised to find that he was where he was, then slumped. 'Where are we?'

'I've no idea. I've just been following the main route towards Toulouse.'

'No need to sound so cross.' Straightening, easing himself upright, he glanced at his watch. 'Five—we should be there soon.' Twisting round, he glanced at Ammy. 'Still asleep,' he murmured softly. Turning back, he winced as he knocked his shoulder, flicked her a glance. Awaiting reproof? 'Tired?'

'A bit.'

'Then stop when you're ready.'

'I will,' she returned decisively, and he laughed.

'That's it, Vina, go down fighting.'

'Down?' she queried tartly. 'I don't intend to go *down*. How are your injuries?'

'Fine.'

'Such a brave soldier,' she mocked.

'Mmm, Captain Courageous, that's me.'

She gave a reluctant smile, and as they entered the outskirts of the town looked for signs to the railway station. When they reached it she drew up outside.

'I'll go and make enquiries,' he murmured with a wry glance. 'Shall I?'

'Yes,' she agreed firmly, and his smile widened.

'Hard-hearted Hannah,' he mocked. Climbing out, he walked into the imposing structure ahead of them, and she sighed. It was best, she told herself. He could get the train back, a car train if he was lucky, or if not he could arrange to have his car collected later, and she could go on to the nearest airport, fly home. It just didn't *feel* best.

He wasn't gone very long—ten minutes or so—and she watched him, tried to be objective about him. It was hard to believe, seeing him now, that they'd made love, been passionately entwined. And it had been passionate. As it could be again—with someone else, she insisted to herself. He was favouring his left arm, holding it against his chest, and she wondered just how much pain he was in.

'The car train doesn't go from here,' he told her quietly as he climbed back in beside her, 'but there's an express to Paris; we could change there for the boat train.'

'And the car?'

'It would have to be left here, collected later—unless you want to use it,' he tacked on.

'What time's the express?'

'Ten.'

'Which means you'd have to spend the night in Paris... Oh.' With a little tut, she switched on the engine. 'I'll drive you to the coast.'

'Thank you. But not tonight.'

'Joel——'

'Because you're too tired. And shocked.'

'No, I'm not, and I'd prefer to go on.'

'Then we'll stop for tea.'

With a little shrug, feeling stupid, outmanoeuvred, she shoved the gear lever into drive, and, once clear of the town, began looking for somewhere to stop.

'Over there,' he said quietly.

'What?'

He pointed, and she nodded as she saw the hoarding on their right advertising a hotel. Indicating to turn off, she followed the signs, then drove through high double wrought-iron gates. Braking involuntarily, she stared in astonishment. 'This is a *hotel*? The palace at Versailles I could believe, but a hotel?' A long carriage drive unfolded before them, and standing proudly at the end was a very, very, stately pile. 'The Duke of Aquitaine?' she quipped. 'Drop in for tea?'

'Just move,' he ordered softly.

'Here?' she asked uncertainly.

'Certainly here.'

Releasing the brake, she did as she was told. 'They won't let us in,' she warned. After glancing at Joel, seeing the stubble that was beginning to darken his jaw, taking in the dusty black clothing, now sadly crumpled as well, she turned her glance on herself, and gave a rueful grimace. 'We look like the *hoi polloi*.'

'*You* might look like the *hoi polloi*,' he argued, '*I* look aristocratic. It is *frequently* remarked upon.'

Yes, it probably was, even though she knew he'd been joking. He *did* look aristocratic. Not that she had any intention of adding to his conceit. With a little snort, she drove on, and pulled up on the fancy gravel beside the magnificent portico. A minion appeared as if by magic, conjured by some unseen hand, dressed in scarlet livery, with a pillbox hat that looked exceedingly silly above his weather-beaten face. He bowed, didn't quite catch his grin in time, and opened Davina's door. '*Madame*,' he intoned.

She gave him a weak smile and obediently alighted. Joel followed, opened the rear door, smiled as Ammy opened her eyes.

'Awake, sweetheart?'

''Wake,' she agreed sleepily, gave a wide yawn to prove it, and then held out her arms.

He unbuckled her, tried to get her out one-handed, and Davina hurried round to help. Smiling at the little girl, she lifted her into her arms, enjoyed again the feel of her warm body, the soft arm encircling her neck. Joel handed the car keys to the liveried footman so that he could park the car, and then urged her inside.

A veritable sea of red carpet confronted them, as well as gilt baroque work, plush furniture, impressive chandeliers. Totally unfazed, probably used to such opulence, Joel walked across to the desk, and it became very obvious that he was not arranging for afternoon tea.

'Joel! I *told* you...' she began furiously as he signed the registration card.

'And I told you that it was too far.' He turned his head, met her concerned eyes. 'So we will stay the night here. Staying,' he emphasised. 'Nothing else. You made it very clear there was to be no—liaison. As did I.'

'I wasn't talking about that,' she denied angrily, 'I was talking about your arbitrary behaviour in over-ruling... I'm perfectly capable of deciding...' Aware that the desk clerk was listening, she bit her lip, gave him a furious glance and stalked after the page-boy and into the lift. She was *perfectly* capable of driving on to the coast, and meant to give Joel a piece of her mind as soon as they were alone.

Within minutes, they were whisked up to the third floor, to pale green carpet, silver-grey walls, diffused lighting—discretion in everything, but no row of doors proclaiming rooms.

'Walk,' Ammy suddenly announced, and Davina put her down.

'She obviously approves,' she murmured, still stiff, and cross, as they followed the page along the hushed corridor to a double set of doors at one end. But then Ammy, like Joel, was probably used to all this. The page manipulated the key, then thrust the doors wide with a practised flourish.

'Suite Royale,' he announced, as though ushering scruffy visitors into such opulence were an everyday occurrence.

Keeping her mouth closed, her tongue very firmly be-tween her teeth until they should be alone, Davina walked somewhat dazedly in. Heavy cream drapes hung in in-tricate folds at the long, wide windows; floor-length snowy nets wafted gently in the breeze from a partially open casement. The carpet was eau-de-Nil, the long sofa and two easy-chairs, upholstered in the same material as the curtains, guarded a low oval, highly polished coffee-table, the requisite bowl of flowers positioned in its centre. There was a matching dining-table and four chairs, an exquisite desk—and then the page was off again, presumably only having waited long enough for the guests to approve the décor of the lounge, before flinging open one of the doors in the far corner. A bedroom *en suite*, naturally, Davina discovered—on her own, because Joel had succumbed to the comfort of the sofa and the page had loped off to the other bedroom.

He patiently awaited her arrival in the second room, then her approval, and when she had nodded in a rather bewildered sort of way, tried a hesitant, '*Très bien*,' she was rewarded with a bow.

The luggage arrived, was deposited, as laconically directed by Joel, in the bedrooms, an enquiry was made as to whether *madame* required the services of a maid, and was declined, the various minions were generously tipped, and a soft silence descended.

Striving for normality, she said quietly, 'And not by the smallest look did they show their scorn.'

'Well-bred,' Joel drawled without opening his eyes.

'Well-*trained*,' she corrected him, thinking that they were probably able to smell money a mile off. 'You said we were coming here for *tea*!'

'Did I?'

'Yes!'

'Bounce,' Ammy announced loudly. Perhaps three-year-olds needed to fill the silences the same way adults did, Davina mused.

'Take your shoes off, then,' Joel ordered, his voice still soft, eyes still closed. 'Sitting bouncing, not standing bouncing, and be careful. Don't fall off.'

'Not fall off,' Ammy agreed obediently as she sat to drag off her shoes.

'Do you need the loo?'

'No,' she said firmly as she toddled off to try out the bouncing propensities of the beds.

'Joel——' Davina began determinedly, only to be interrupted.

'Don't,' he said as he reluctantly opened his eyes. 'Only a fool drives beyond their capabilities—and no, I'm not deriding your driving. You narrowly escaped a nasty accident this morning, and although you might not think it you're still shocked. You then had to cope with the pass, which is not easy when you're relaxed, let alone stressed——'

'I was not stressed,' she automatically denied.

'——and so this seemed the obvious solution, and I can hardly cause you—trouble, can I? Even if I wanted to...'

'Which you don't.'

'Which I don't,' he agreed, 'and, even if I did, a determined two-year-old, one hand tied behind his back could defeat me. And it's entirely irrational, you know,' he continued, just the faintest trace of amusement in his eyes. 'Refusing to speak to me, acknowledge me, won't take away what happened. I've already told you there'll be no pursuit, and, that being so, wouldn't it make more sense to be friends?'

Friends? With Joel Gilman? 'Don't be absurd,' she dismissed without thinking. 'You aren't the sort of man women are *friends* with!'

'Then be my lover.'

'No! And you just finished telling me——'

'Only not today,' he continued softly as though she hadn't spoken. 'Today I don't think I could manage it.'

'Joel! Stop being absurd!'

'Is it absurd? Why?'

'You know why! Because...'

'Because you're engaged? Or because I took your virginity?' he asked, oh, so softly. 'In a bathroom?'

CHAPTER FOUR

'JOEL!' Davina protested in horror. Glancing quickly round to make sure that Ammy wasn't listening, she gave him a look of reproof. 'There are some things you just *don't* say!'

'Are there? Bathroom being one of them?'

'No!'

'Virginity? Why? Everyone has it, everyone—or nearly everyone—loses it. You should consider yourself lucky you lost it to an—expert.' His smile was mocking, and then he asked unexpectedly, 'Why don't you wear a ring?'

'What?' she asked blankly.

'Ring, Davina, as in "I am an engaged lady".'

'Because—because,' she floundered, 'we haven't chosen it yet! And don't change the subject!'

'I wasn't; I was merely trying to reassure you that your—er—virtue was safe. Or don't you want it to be safe?' he asked after the tiniest of pauses.

'Yes!'

'Then why the argument? A suite seemed the obvious solution. I'm not taking advantage of your good nature, or at least I am, but I really don't think I could cope adequately with Ammy with my arm out of action. I could get a maid in to take care of her, but——'

'No!' she broke in impatiently. 'And that wasn't what I was going to say before you side-tracked me! I wasn't about to complain about the arrangements.' Weren't you, Davina? Weren't you really? 'I'm not a complete fool,' she added quickly. 'I can see you're in pain. I was only querying your overriding of my abilities—and the expense!' she tacked on.

'Expense?' he asked, as though the word didn't exist in his vocabulary, which it probably didn't. 'You mean the cost of the suite?'

'Well, of course that's what I mean!'

He made a little negative movement with his hand. 'Don't worry, we won't have to do a runner.' Continuing to watch her, he asked quietly, 'What is it about me that frightens you so much, Davina?'

'Nothing; don't be ridiculous. Go and lie down.'

'With you?'

'No! And stop flirting with me! It doesn't mean anything, does it? You do it without thought, without meaning, because you arrogantly think that's what women want!'

'Do I?'

'Yes. And what you seem to forget is that I'm no longer twenty-two. No longer naïve, no longer accepting the glib explanations offered me and, that being so, I understand very well why you pursued me in Andorra!'

'Do you? Because I thought you wanted to be pursued? The way you wanted to be pursued four years ago?'

'I did not! And anyway,' she added confusingly, 'I thought you were unattached.'

'I was.'

'Oh, yes, *so* unattached,' she scoffed, 'that two days after meeting me you went back to her!'

'And that rankles, doesn't it?'

'Of course it rankles! I'd just been rejected by Paul...'

'And a few weeks later rejected by me? But you didn't want me, did you? You wanted Paul. I was merely a body to punish, wasn't I? Wasn't I?' he persisted softly.

'Yes.' Trapped by her own stupidity, she turned away.

He got to his feet, walked up behind her, turned her round. 'Wasn't I?'

Unable to mask her feelings in time, she bit her lip, and he swore.

'Davina, I returned to Celia because she discovered she was pregnant,' he said quietly.

She gave a bitterly ironic smile. So was I, she wanted to tell him. 'And if she hadn't been?'

'I don't know.'

'Did you love her?'

He sighed. 'Not in the accepted sense. Not the grand passion, not what you would probably call love, but I was fond of her, thought for a while she was what I wanted, needed; but Celia had her own emotional hang-ups. Rank feminism being one of them,' he added with a twisted smile. 'She ordered her life, and I was only an incidental part of it——'

'Like you were to your mother?' she put in softly.

He looked surprised for a moment, and then shrugged. 'Maybe, but once she discovered that she couldn't control or direct my talent... *Did* you want me to stay?'

She shook her head, because she hadn't—then.

'Expect it?' he persisted.

Hesitating, she shook her head again.

'Then why did you come to find me?' he queried softly.

Snapping up her head, she stared at him. 'I didn't!'

'Then how did you know I was back with Celia two days after I left you?'

'Because...'

'Because you did come? Why?'

To see you. To try and make sense of muddled feelings. To tell you I was pregnant. Searching his face, her own eyes wide and troubled, she knew she could say none of it. 'To apologise,' she fabricated.

'Apologise?' For a moment he looked—doubtful, and then asked, 'That was the only reason?'

'Yes,' she insisted. 'I was ashamed of my behaviour, and came to apologise.'

'But you didn't.'

'No. I wasn't sure of the number of your house and I stopped to ask someone, a man doing someone's garden. "Celia and Joel?" he queried. "Yes, of course, they live at number thirty-two." *They*,' she emphasised softly, 'and I did ask him, to be sure, whether Celia was there with you...'

'And he confirmed it?'

'Yes, he said he thought he'd seen you go out, but that your wife was there. Celia.'

'And so you went away without knocking.'

'Yes.' Muddled and confused and hurting—and so very afraid. 'I asked him if he knew how long you'd lived there,' she whispered, 'and he told me.' He was the sort of man who knew everything. It was a private estate, where everyone knew all about their neighbours.

'And he told you that I'd moved back two days after I'd left you,' he nodded. 'And so you felt doubly rejected.'

Well, it wouldn't hurt to admit that, she supposed. 'Yes. I loved Paul, but I'd never *made* love to him, so my feelings for you, for the way you'd made me feel, were confusing. I assumed, I suppose, that making love to Paul would have felt the same...'

'And have since found out differently,' he stated.

'Yes—no—I mean, not with Paul.'

'Of course not,' he mocked. 'I meant with others.'

'Yes,' she lied, before rushing on quickly, 'and, although I told you to go, later I felt ashamed—but when I discovered you'd immediately gone back to Celia I felt—cheated,' she whispered, 'as though I hadn't even been worth...'

'A few weeks of celibacy?'

'Something like that. Oh, this is so pointless!' she cried. 'We met again by accident, and you thought I'd be an easy option, that's all it was!'

'Was it?'

'Yes,' she said positively. 'You thought it might be amusing, for whatever warped reason you have. You don't want me, see me as a person, do you?'

'Don't I?'

'No. And don't keep answering questions with questions! I'm just the girl whose virginity you took, and perhaps...'

'Perhaps?'

Her mouth tight, she snapped, 'If it wasn't to pay me back, then perhaps you saw me as your property!'

'Property?' he asked in astonishment.

'Yes! But all it boils down to is that we made love——'

'Had sex,' he corrected her.

'All right, had sex—in a bathroom! You took me home and stayed the night. Celia beckoned, and back you went to your shackles.'

'Because she was pregnant.'

'Yes, because she was pregnant.'

'You don't believe me?'

'It doesn't *matter* what I believe! Does it?'

'No,' he agreed thoughtfully. 'You were hurt, used me to ease the pain, and really that's all it was, isn't it? The rest is just window-dressing. Although I'm sorry you felt rejected.'

'Are you?' Rejected? She had felt mortified. It had festered inside her like a canker, and when she'd miscarried it had felt like the final blow. Her mother's illness had seemed like a lifeline to sanity, and from there pride and shame and misery had dictated that she change her life, grow a hard outer shell where no pain could filter through ever again. And over the years, she suddenly realised, she had come to blame Joel for all the ills that ever befell her. And by the same token, she thought with even more surprise, shouldn't he therefore be praised for making her the success she now was? Confused and aching, wishing there were simple answers to life's problems, and realising that he hadn't actually answered anything she had asked him, that he probably never would, never tell her how he had felt about it all, she knew she must not let him get any closer, re-direct her life for a second time. 'Go and get some sleep,' she concluded with a tired sigh.

His nod was accepting, as though none of it really mattered. Which it probably didn't—to him. 'Could you order Ammy something to eat? We can go down for a meal later.'

'I'll order us all something to eat. You don't look as though you're going anywhere in a hurry.'

'True, oh, bossy one.' Waving a languid hand, he walked carefully into the master bedroom, closed the door, and then opened it again. 'You don't need to *hide* here, Davina, and you certainly don't need to feel inadequate——'

'I don't,' she interrupted.

'Good; you have no need to blush for your manners, which are impeccable, you know which knife and fork to use, your background is acceptable...'

'I know that!'

'And even if it weren't, there is absolutely no need to feel intimidated.'

'I do not feel intimidated!'

'Then feel free to wander. And if anyone looks at you with superior derision, tell them to——'

'I shan't tell them anything!'

He smiled, and closed the door.

'And neither am I bossy!' she muttered. She hadn't been behaving that way because she couldn't cope with staying in a fancy hotel, but because she couldn't cope with *him*! She'd been working on the assumption that if she tried hard enough she *could* handle him, handle her feelings, and had found that she could do neither. The truth was, she didn't *know* him. Had *never* known him. Her reading of his character had been based on hearsay. All she really knew about him was his body, how he could affect her emotions, and that was very shaky ground indeed. And yet she *felt* as though she knew him. She also suspected that she was right about his flirting, because it came as natural as breathing to him, because he thought women expected and wanted it. He probably didn't know he was doing it half the time.

Feeling depressed and bewildered, as though her life was no longer hers to control, she also wondered if he'd lied about the train service. So why didn't you ask him, Davina? Because this is what you *really* wanted? No, but she did think she needed to take a long, hard look at herself, make a decision about future relationships, because she didn't think she could go on as she was.

Walking across to the desk, she hunted in the drawers for the hotel brochure, then looked up the number for Room Service. Ordering a child's meal and something cold for herself and Joel, she went to see what mischief Ammy was getting up to.

When she'd eaten, and leaving Ammy to finish hers, Davina tiptoed into Joel's room to rescue Ammy's suitcase, and then just stood staring down at him for a moment. He lay on top of the bed, fully clothed, only his shoes removed, his sleep uneasy, and his left hand twitching spasmodically as though it hurt. Finding a spare blanket in the top of the wardrobe, she gently covered him, picked up Ammy's small case and went quietly out.

'All done,' Ammy announced cheerfully, and Davina smiled.

'There's a good girl. You *were* hungry, weren't you?'

'Yes,' she agreed happily. 'Swings.'

'Swings? I don't think there are any, poppet. We could go for a walk...'

'Walk,' Ammy agreed with her funny little nod. Feeling rather restless herself, and guessing that Ammy wouldn't yet be tired after her long sleep that afternoon, Davina tidied them both, collected the room key, and with Ammy held firmly by one hand they went to investigate their immediate surroundings. They found the nearby village, where ice-cream was duly bought, looked in the few shops, and then took a slow walk back with Ammy chattering happily about her day.

Davina quickly checked on Joel when they got back, and, finding him still asleep, quietly closed his door.

'Bath now,' Ammy announced.

'Bath?'

'Yes. Bubbles.'

'Oh, right.' Obviously a child who knew what she wanted from life—and expected to get it. Just like her father. Following her into the bedroom, and then into their own *en-suite* bathroom, Davina smiled as Ammy began shedding her clothes. Fitting in the plug and turning on the taps, she ran about a foot of water before deciding it was deep enough. Investigating the various sachets placed in a delicately sculpted bowl, she found bubble bath and emptied it into the water. Suddenly remembering all those tales she'd heard over the years, unconsciously picked up 'what to dos', and feeling a bit silly, she tested the water with her elbow. Not convinced, terrified that Ammy would burn herself, she tested it with her other elbow, then her foot. Ammy watched her as though it was a ritual that one must take seriously.

When she was satisfied that Ammy wouldn't get scalded, Davina helped her in.

'All right?'

She beamed. 'Ammy got bubbles,' she announced with her funny little nod. 'Ammy laughing.'

'Yes, Ammy laughing.' Delighted, a warm smile curving her mouth, Davina began to soap her warm little body, played find-the-soap with her, played splashing. Only then, of course, Ammy didn't want to get out.

'You'll get cold,' Davina warned.

'Cold,' Ammy agreed, unperturbed.

'And it's bedtime.'

'Bedtime,' she nodded as she continued to play with the diminishing bubbles.

'Ammy...' She was given a crafty sideways look. 'You're a little monkey.' Ammy giggled.

Leaning forward, Davina pulled out the plug, stifled Ammy's wail of protest by lifting her out, wrapping her in a towel and tickling her. 'Bed.' Davina then said firmly.

Carrying her into the bedroom, she dumped Ammy playfully on the double bed and opened the suitcase to find her pyjamas—which seemed to signal a chase. It was obviously a nightly ritual, because Ammy laughed and raced off into the lounge. By the time she'd caught her, forced her wriggling body into the pyjamas, Davina felt exhausted.

'Daddy.'

'Daddy sleeping.'

'See.'

Staring down into the little girl's face, Davina nodded. 'You have to be very quiet, though, not wake him up.'

'Not wake him up,' she agreed, and put a finger to her lips for good measure. Tiptoeing exaggeratedly, she opened Joel's door and peeped inside, then smiled. 'Daddy 'sleep.'

'Yes.'

She walked quietly over to the bed, scrambled on top, and pressed a kiss to his cheek. He stirred, mumbled something, and Ammy scrambled down, smiled at Davina, and went back into the other room. Climbing into the single bed, she beamed. 'Story.'

Oh, lord. Tucking the little girl in, Davina perched on the edge of the bed, and began, 'Once upon a time...'

'Read it.'

'We don't have a book.'

'Read it,' she repeated. Very firmly.

'Please,' Davina prompted.

'Please.'

With a helpless nod, and recalling the bookcase in the lounge, Davina went to see if there was anything suitable for a child. They were mostly discarded paperbacks, but one was a book on birds. The text was in French, but there were plenty of pictures. Picking it up, she returned to the bedroom, sat beside Ammy and opened it at the first page.

'What's that?' Ammy demanded, pointing.

'You tell me.'

'Duck. Quack, quack,' she said with a grin, and as though it was a joke. Perhaps it was. Perhaps it was a game she played with Joel, or her mother.

They progressed through seagulls, puffins, garden birds, and then came to the birds of prey, and perhaps because they were big, or looked important, or reminded her of the stone griffins that stood outside the hotel in Andorra, that was the page Ammy wanted read. One of the eagles was carrying a worm in its beak, for which Davina was extremely thankful. It could have been a poor little mouse. The eagle next to it was looking decidedly disapproving, and Davina smiled, and quickly invented some words for him.

'*Excuse* me!' she exclaimed in what she hoped might sound like a fierce, eagle-type voice. 'But can I have my *worm* back? I've had no dinner, no tea, and I'm very, very hungry!'

'Very, very hungry,' Ammy nodded. 'No dinner, no tea...'

'No, that's right! Naughty eagle.'

'And won't give it back!' Ammy agreed with that funny little shake of her head. 'Can I have my worm back?'

'Yes, because you mustn't take things that belong to other people, must you?'

'No, it's naughty. What's his name?'

'Ernie.'

'Ernie,' Ammy agreed with a firm nod.

'And that's—um—Clarence.'

Ammy pointed to the eagle at the top of the page. 'Aunt Mildred,' Davina said obediently. The little finger moved on. 'Uncle John—and Bessie.'

'Bessie. Read.'

'Please.'

'Please.'

Four pages later, all the birds having now been named, Ammy's eyelids began to close, and Davina tucked her in, gently kissed her cheek, and very thankfully closed the book. A faint smile on her mouth and, had she known it, a very loving expression in her eyes, she quietly put the book on the bedside table, and went to have a shower.

It was hardly worth dressing, so she pulled on her pyjamas and dressing-gown, and walked into the lounge. Moving to the window, she hooked back the net and stared down at the immaculately sculpted garden at the rear of the hotel. An elderly couple were touring the flowerbeds, pointing things out to each other, the flowers far more advanced this far south than they were in her own garden at home. Guests, she supposed, taking a little stroll before enjoying their dinner. With a sigh, feeling restless, she allowed the curtain to drop back in place. It was only nine o'clock, far too early to go to bed, even if she'd been tired, which she wasn't. She should have been, but her mind was too churned up to allow her to sleep.

Barely aware of what she was doing, she eased open Joel's door and peered in at him. He lay as he had earlier, hair tousled across his forehead, the blanket still covering him, and she felt that funny little dip in her stomach. She wanted to walk across, smooth his tousled hair, climb in beside him, fit herself along that warm body; she remembered so very vividly how it had felt. And if she

did, what sort of heartache would she be letting herself
in for? He's not for you, Davina, she told herself firmly.
No. She might wish he were, but it was best to be sensible. It didn't stop the ache, though. Or the yearning.

Gently closing the door, she wandered back to the
window. She ought to ring Michael, let him know of her
change in plans, that she'd be back later than intended.
He would want to know how the tour had gone, how
she'd managed, but she didn't feel like talking to him,
explaining. With another long sigh, she went to investigate the paperbacks in the bookcase, and at ten o'clock,
the book she'd chosen barely broached, she leaned back
on the comfortable sofa, letting her mind drift. It was
safer for him to be sleeping. If he'd been awake... You
don't want him awake, Davina, really you don't, an inner
voice told her. But she did, could feel all her resolutions
slipping, and that was so damned stupid. Snapping the
book shut, she went quickly into her bedroom, firmly
closing the door. Checking that Ammy was all right, she
quietly closed the curtains and climbed into the
comfortable bed. Everything would probably look better
in the morning...

The gentle click of the door opening woke her with a
start. Alarmed, she stared round her at the unfamiliar
room, then slumped tiredly as memory rushed back.
'Joel?' she whispered, and as she said his name sweet
excitement flooded her.

'Sorry,' he murmured, 'I didn't mean to wake you.
Ammy OK?'

'Yes, she's fine.'

'All right. Go back to sleep.'

Sleep? What did you expect, Davina? That he would
join you? No! She could hear him in the lounge, imagined him wandering aimlessly back and forth, heard

the soft ping as he lifted the phone. Hungry perhaps, aching, and knowing she shouldn't, knowing she was being a fool, she slipped quietly from the bed, shrugged into her dressing-gown, and moved silently out of the room and into the lounge. Weak sunlight was probing through the wide windows, and she frowned, yawned. Joel was standing as she'd been earlier, staring out at the grounds. He looked like someone she wanted to hug. You should have stayed in bed, Davina. Yes. You should be avoiding this situation. 'What time is it?' she asked quietly.

'Six,' he answered without consulting his watch—and without seeming surprised that she was there.

'How do you feel?'

'Lousy,' he murmured without turning. 'I've just ordered up some coffee.'

'And something to eat? I ordered you something last night, but...'

'No.'

'You should——' she began worriedly.

'Don't,' he bit out. Allowing the net to fall back into place, he turned, and Davina drew in a sharp breath. 'Oh, Joel, your poor face. It's awfully swollen.'

'Tell me something I don't know,' he murmured almost absently as he stared at her, took her in from her bare toes to her tousled hair. His eyes looked extraordinarily bright. 'You should have stayed in bed.'

'Yes,' she agreed, and her voice sounded husky, unsure. 'So should you. Two steps away from a mortuary slab is how you look.'

'I'm all right. I'm going to have a shower,' he added brusquely as he moved back towards his bedroom. 'Let the waiter in when he comes.'

'All right.' Feeling ever so slightly wrung out, she plumped down in one of the comfortable chairs, waited for the waiter. She knew she should go and get dressed before he came back, but she didn't want to, didn't have the energy, or the inclination. You're playing with fire, Davina, she told herself. Yes. A death-wish... but there was a little curl of excitement in her tummy, a pleasurable pain. You only want him because he doesn't want you. No! No. When the soft knock came on the door, she jumped, hurried to answer it, indicated for the waiter to put the tray on the coffee-table, realised she didn't have any francs with which to tip him, and gave him a helpless look. He smiled, shook his head, and quietly left.

Sitting on the sofa, nerves screwing her muscles tight, she poured herself a coffee, gratefully sipped the hot liquid and, when Joel padded out, glanced at him nervously. She took in the wet hair, the freshly shaved chin, the short-sleeved blue shirt that hung unbuttoned on his slim frame, the loose navy trousers, his bare feet, and quickly changed her mind. Putting her cup down, she jumped to her feet. 'I'd better go and get dressed.'

'Too late,' he said softly as he deliberately moved his gaze to the open neck of her robe.

'No...'

'Yes. Pour me some coffee, would you? Black, no sugar.'

Her movements jerky, she sat on the edge of the chair behind her, poured his coffee and handed it to him. The cup rattled in the saucer. 'Did the doctor give you anything for your face?'

'Mmm, yellow paint. It's on the dressing-table in my room.' Easing himself into the chair opposite, his cup held in his good hand, his eyes steady on hers, he leaned back. 'Ammy go to bed all right?'

'Yes.'

'Thank you.'

'You're welcome.'

He smiled. 'Come here.'

'No. I have to go and get dressed.'

He shook his head. 'I'm not a man to play games with, Davina.'

'I'm not playing games,' she denied quickly, huskily.

'Aren't you?'

'No. I was worried about you. I . . . And stop shaking your head at me! You don't know what I think! Feel!'

'Oh, but I do. If I didn't, I would be extremely angry, because I would think you were deliberately teasing.'

'Well, I'm not!'

'No,' he agreed, still gently, 'you're confused, but if it makes you happier by all means go and get dressed.'

She did. Almost ran to do so—and only just remembered in time to close the door quietly. With the curtains still drawn she could just make out the slight hump of Ammy's little body under the covers, hear her soft breathing, and just for a moment was tempted to wake her, use her as a shield. You're being absurd, Davina, she scolded herself. Stupid and childish and ridiculous. He doesn't want you; he said so—no, he didn't; he said he wouldn't pursue you—unless you gave him encouragement. Which you aren't going to do, so why is there a horrid little fluttering in your stomach? A pain in your throat? Why are you behaving in this ridiculously contrary fashion?

Quietly collecting clean underwear and clothes, she padded into the bathroom to wash. Five minutes later, dressed in comfortable brown trousers and a cream silk shirt that buttoned to the neck, she returned to the lounge. He was sitting exactly where she'd left him, head back, eyes closed, the coffee still held in one hand, and she fiercely suppressed the desire to go to him.

'Where's this stuff I have to paint you with?' she asked abruptly.

'On the dressing-table, I told you,' he answered without moving, but there was a faint smile on his mouth which awoke very violent feelings in her breast. He was *enjoying* her discomfort!

'Sadist,' she muttered as she went to get the bottle. The label, naturally, was printed in French, which she couldn't read, and she was forced to ask, 'What does it say?'

'Apply as required,' he drawled.

She bet it didn't. Bet he hadn't even read it. Unscrewing the top, she went to stand beside him, looked with alarm at the angry graze, the swollen flesh, felt a supreme reluctance actually to touch it. It was going to hurt like hell.

'Just do it, Davina,' he ordered softly, still without opening his eyes.

'Did you wash it when you had your shower?'

'No. Do I look like a masochist?'

Her mouth pursed, she withdrew the little brush from the bottle, stared rather dubiously at the thick yellow liquid, and tentatively touched it to his temple.

'Ow!' he yelled, making her jump.

'Well, you told me to do it!' she snapped defensively. 'And I can't do it if I don't touch you!'

His eyes bright, exasperated, yet still with that touch of humour, he removed the bottle from her hand and ordered softly, 'Go and find me a mirror.'

Striding across to the wall by the bookcase, she unhooked the small gilt-framed mirror that hung there and took it back. Perching on the edge of the coffee-table in front of him, she held it on her knees so that he could see what he was doing, then hissed in sympathy when he gingerly applied the brush to his face.

'It probably doesn't need doing...' he began as he withdrew the brush.

'Yes, it does!' she insisted. 'Don't be a baby; just get on with it.'

'Oh, we are brave all of a sudden,' he retorted, 'and it's not your damned face that feels as though it's been branded!'

'Then you shouldn't have played the hero! For God's sake, Joel, you bungy-jump off tall buildings!'

'Jumped,' he corrected her. 'Twice. For charity. And let me tell you it was a damned sight less painful than this! Oh, you do it!' Thrusting the bottle back at her, he grabbed the mirror with his good hand, and waited stoically for her to begin.

'Stop hissing,' he ordered as she carefully painted his face. 'I'm the one being tortured. And don't *dab* it!' Grasping her wrist, he halted a movement of determined bravado, and cautioned softly, 'Gently.'

Holding his eyes, she was the first to look away, and he slowly released her wrist, allowed her to finish.

'And how, my little friend,' he asked softly, 'do you know I went bungy-jumping? I thought you weren't interested in what I did?'

'I'm not. I read it somewhere,' she muttered defiantly as she screwed the top back on the bottle. 'How does it feel now?'

'Fine.'

'You look like a clown.'

'Good. I'll go down to breakfast juggling.'

'Very amusing. How's your shoulder?'

'Sore. And if you tell me I should have left the sling on, I'll probably hit you.'

'Do, and I'll hit you right back,' she warned, knowing full well that he would never lay a hand on a woman. Not in anger, anyway. He gave a slow smile, and she looked away quickly. 'You should see a doctor.'

'I'll go when I get home.' Lowering the mirror, he leaned it against the coffee-table, returned his eyes to hers, then glanced down at the high-buttoned shirt, and his lips twitched. 'You can go *too* far you know.'

'Can you?' she asked, unmollified.

'Mmm, and if you think that a high-buttoned shirt makes you less desirable, let me tell you that it doesn't.' As he reached forward to undo the top button, Davina slapped his hand away—too late.

'Now who's playing games?'

He continued to stare at her. 'Blow hot, blow cold, is that it?'

'No,' she replied stonily.

'Then why?' he asked more gently. 'Because you don't know what you want? Or because you want it all taken out of your hands?'

'No, I don't want anything.' Pressing her hands to the table on either side of her, she tried to rise, but his hand on her shoulder prevented her.

'Always been this muddled, have you?' he asked even more gently. 'Or only since Paul?'

Looking down, she refused to answer. She knew she was doing all the things he said she was doing—only she didn't know how to stop. There was a crazy sort of excitement in these verbal games, and perhaps part of her did want him to resolve it, take it out of her hands.

'Poor Davina,' he mocked softly.

'It wouldn't be "poor Davina" if you hadn't...'

'Aroused you? Tormented you? Painted a little picture with words? Is that what Michael does?'

'No.'

'And will you tell him about—this?'

'There's nothing to tell.'

'Yet,' he said softly.

'At all!' she insisted firmly. 'Look, I only...'

'Funny word, that, isn't it? *Only*. Useful.'

'Yes,' she agreed defiantly. 'I'll go and see if Ammy is awa—— Joel,' she warned, 'let go of my arm.'

He increased the pressure on her wrist, pulled her gently but insistently towards him.

'Joel! If I fall on you, you'll have no one to blame but yourself if I hurt your injuries.'

'Then kneel.'

'No!' she exclaimed, shocked, but he pulled her off balance anyway and she ended up right where he wanted her, on her knees. Where she wanted to be, if she'd had the courage to admit it. But the feel of him so close frightened her, and she clamped her free hand above his knee with the intention of levering herself upright, became unbearably aware of the strong muscles beneath her hand, the warmth of him, the sheer masculinity. Struggling, she wrenched her wrist free of his hand, and then wished she'd stayed still because, his good hand now free, he curved it round her neck, urged her closer. His mouth almost touching hers, she stared pleadingly up into his blue eyes, tried to breathe. 'Don't do this, Joel,' she begged. 'Please don't.'

Ignoring her plea, he said quietly, 'Your eyes say no, but your body says yes—and I think you have to be the loveliest woman I've ever met. Not beautiful, not in the classical sense, but such wonderful bones.' Careful of his injury, he awkwardly lifted his free hand, touched his fingers to her cheekbones, her nose, her mouth, and then down to the edge of her collar, tracing the opening of her shirt, his fingers trailing as he slipped another button free. His mouth was a sensuous line, and she felt entirely incapable of moving away.

'You're shivering. Are you afraid of me, Davina?'

'Yes,' she whispered hoarsely.

'Yes. Emotion is the damnedest thing, isn't it? Hits without warning, curls in the stomach, unfreezes muscles until you feel pliable, soft—wanting. I've dreamed of your mouth on mine, the feel of you, the taste of you, the little noises you make when you're being—loved. Full breasts that fit a man's hand to perfection, the way your tongue——'

'Oh, dear God,' she groaned. Helpless, mesmerised, such a feeling of overwhelming need inside her, she rested her cheek against his knee, closing her eyes defeatedly. Warmth was spreading throughout her body, filling her, weakening her, setting an ache so deep inside her that she thought nothing would relieve it ever again, and with her eyes closed she drew in the scent of him, the shape of him, and when his fingers moved on her nape, sending a long shiver through her, she raised her face, helplessly sought what she had wanted for such a very long time. His mouth was gentle as it closed over hers, the fingers that had traced her bones like butterfly wings as they trailed to her jaw, probed the sensitive hollow beneath her ear. Dazed, wanting, allowing her mouth to be manipulated by his, she moved her arm to his waist, slid it slowly round him, held him closer. Reciprocal emotion, a perfect half, a perfect self, and more than anything in the world this was what she wanted. To be held by him, loved by him, to taste, touch, feel every inch of him.

'Like coming home,' he murmured hoarsely.

'Yes,' she agreed thickly. And it was.

'Then stop fighting it. We could love. Oh, Davina, how we could love.'

A sound that was almost a sob escaped her as her fingers edged towards his groin, and she thought her lungs would burst with the sheer effort it took to breathe. Her head far too heavy for her slender neck, it tipped backwards, exposing her long throat—and then she jerked in shock, would have toppled backwards had the coffee-table not been at her back, as the bedroom door slammed open behind her with a crash that would have shaken a lesser hotel.

'Ammy awake!'

Davina scrambled free, her senses in turmoil, and whirled round to stare somewhat blankly at the little girl, standing with her raggedy doll trailing from one hand. Warm and flushed from sleep, she stood there beaming.

'*Excuse* me!' she announced happily. 'Haven't had no dinner, haven't had no tea!'

'Oh, Ammy!' Davina exclaimed helplessly. Not daring to look at Joel, who she knew was bending forward, his arm across his knees, head bent, laughing, she walked unsteadily to intercept the little girl, giving Joel time to recover. 'Did you have a good sleep?'

Ammy blinked, looked as though she couldn't imagine why anyone should think she hadn't, dodged round Davina, and went to stand beside Joel.

'Daddy better,' she announced firmly, as though it would automatically set her world back to rights.

'Daddy better,' he agreed as he raised his head, stared at her wryly, his blue eyes just a little too bright.

'All yellow.'

'Yes, sweetheart, all yellow.' As he raised his eyes to Davina, his smile grew and he gave a choked laugh. 'All yellow sounds about right.'

Her face pink, Davina turned away, walked across to the window, stared, without seeing, into the grounds. She wanted him. With every fibre of her being, she wanted him. Was it better for want to go unfulfilled? Or better to give in to it and pray you would not get too badly scarred in the process? No, not in the process. At the end. Because it would end, she knew that, knew he had no real feelings for her...only desire, affection maybe. So was it better never to begin? Life was about chances. You took them, hoped for the best, or you played safe, never took risks—and when you were eighty did you regret such cowardice? Or thank God you'd been sensible?

'Davina?'

Turning, almost surprised to find that she was still in the room with them, her amber eyes wide, she gave herself a little shake, walked back.

'Hungry?'

'Mmm.'

'Restaurant? Or Room Service?'

'Restaurant.' That would be safer, and until she could get herself back on an even keel safe would be best.

The waiter who greeted them at the door of the dining-room was the same man who had greeted them the day before, minus red hat and jacket. The name-tag above the pocket of his white jacket proclaimed him to be Henri. His face did not lend itself to gravity, but he tried.

'There is a shortness of staff,' he explained lugubri-ously with that wonderful Gallic shrug.

Davina's lips twitched, and an appreciative twinkle appeared in his dark brown eyes.

'If you will be so kind?' Leading them towards a small table set in the window, he continued, 'As you will see, we are not busy, so you will 'ave my undivided attention.' He held the chair for Davina, then for Ammy. '*Café*?'

Joel glanced at Davina, who nodded. '*Oui, merci*. Ammy? Juice? Milk?'

'Juice.'

'Please.'

'Please.'

Henri bowed, and, his attention directed exclusively towards the little girl, he asked gravely, 'Would *mademoiselle* like the full breakfast?'

Ammy looked up at him, a hint of calculation in her bright blue eyes, then replied with quiet solemnity, 'No, thank you. I'm on a diet.'

There was a startled pause; Davina snorted, Joel choked, then began to laugh, a warm, enthusiastic, *infectious* laugh, and Davina stared at him, her face soft, eyes full of smiles. She'd never seen him laugh like that, with such full-throated enjoyment, and in that moment of shared affinity if he'd asked her for the moon she would have given it to him.

'Celia,' he gasped. 'She must have heard Celia say it. She's *always* on a diet. Oh, Moppet, you'll be the death of me.'

Ammy beamed happily, a cheeky little grin that would have melted the sternest heart.

His face still creased with amusement, Joel asked, 'What *would* you like?'

And no doubt unwilling to relinquish this heady ability to make people laugh, crack little jokes, she giggled enchantingly. 'Worm. Can I have a *worm*, please?'

Unfazed, his eyes alight with wonderful appreciation, Henri asked solemnly, 'Grilled? Fried?'

'Fried!' she exclaimed happily.

'*Monsieur*? *Madame*?'

'Just croissants for me,' Davina murmured, a little catch of laughter in her throat. Joel nodded, his eyes still on his daughter, his blue eyes full of warmth and love.

'And would *mademoiselle* like to choose 'er worm?' Henri asked, and when Ammy nodded he helped her down and escorted her to the long buffet table.

'She's adorable,' Davina murmured as she watched the slow perambulation to choose or discard from each laid-out dish.

'Yes,' Joel agreed, his face holding an enjoyment to match her own, and when they returned, with a plate laid out to resemble a face, sausage for mouth, button mushrooms for eyes and nose, a spoonful of scrambled egg for hair, Joel smiled warmly at Henri.

'Thank you.'

'*Non*,' he denied, 'thank *you*. Is the most fun I 'ave 'ad all week!'

The coffee and croissants were brought, and in a mood of almost carefree companionship they talked and laughed as old friends, tension for the moment forgotten.

'It's not a *real* worm,' Ammy explained kindly with her funny little nod, presumably just in case they didn't understand the joke.

'No,' Joel agreed lovingly, 'not a real worm.' They smiled at each other, then turned to include Davina in their warmth. A precious little moment to savour. A moment that burrowed into her heart, and would never be dislodged.

They were on the road by ten, and, having had a quick glance at the map, feeling more relaxed and happy about things, Davina queried, 'Dieppe?'

'Caen,' he replied laconically.

'Caen? But Dieppe is a straighter route.'

'Caen,' he repeated.

Puzzled, she gave a little shrug. It made no difference to her, but it seemed an odd choice. 'You're the navigator.'

'Mmm.'

Not entirely understanding his behaviour, but not wanting to make an issue of it, she concentrated on her driving. *Was* he playing with her? A game where she had never known the rules? But she had come through one test—shaken, she thought wryly, but at least un-conquered, and now there would be no need for them to be alone together again. Tonight they would get the ferry, and tomorrow she would be home. And it felt so terribly unsatisfying, especially after the shared warmth of breakfast. And yet, in a way, wasn't it a relief to know what came next? Know that she had met him again, a meeting she had always feared, and emerged relatively unscathed? Knowing she was lying to herself, but not knowing how else to cope, and so unbearably aware of every breath he took, every move he made, everything he said as he chatted to Ammy, she gave a helpless sigh. This time last week she'd been confident, capable, in charge of her life, and now look at her. An emotional wreck. And what did he feel? Nothing? Amusement? Or total indifference? Maybe if there had been other lovers he wouldn't affect her so. But there hadn't been other lovers, and he did affect her. She wanted to smile at him, touch him, be a part of his life. Wanted to have his child.

A child of her own, like Ammy, to make up for that other time.

She saw him glance at his watch, and she asked quietly, 'You want me to drive faster?'

'No, no,' he denied amiably, 'go at your own pace; there's no rush.'

Wasn't there? Because he was enjoying her company? Or only enjoying the scenery? she wondered despondently. And she hated this feeling of insecurity, vulnerability, which she hadn't experienced for a long time, and telling herself she was successful, competent made not the slightest bit of difference. She wanted him; her body wanted him—and it felt as though her wretched hormones were busily making adjustments, just in case.

They stopped for lunch, and then again for dinner just outside Flers, and eventually arrived in Caen in late evening—just in time to miss the ferry.

'I should have driven faster,' she confessed flatly.

'It doesn't matter.'

'Doesn't it?'

'No.'

Her heart beating over-fast, staring into eyes that quietly waited, she whispered, 'Why doesn't it?'

'Because we can find a hotel. Can't we?'

Through a throat that felt closed, she managed, 'Only to sleep.'

'Yes, only to sleep. Over there,' he instructed softly, his hand pointing, but his eyes still on hers.

She nodded, automatically obeyed, drove along to the hotel opposite the port.

'Another suite, if they have one.'

What did that mean? Because it was easier with Ammy? Or...? Fluttering nerves, a flood of feverish need too long denied were robbing her of the ability to speak. Ask. He never spoke in plain language, never said it was this or that and, because she was so inexperienced, she didn't know how to behave. Didn't know if she was reading more into it than there was. Did he really not want her? Much safer not to be wanted, Davina. Yes, but if this was the last time she'd see him did she want to be safer?

'Joel?'

'Mmm?'

Pulling up outside the hotel, carefully setting the handbrake, she gave an abrupt shake of her head. 'Nothing.' She didn't see his smile as she unlatched her door, which was perhaps fortunate.

There wasn't a suite available, so Joel booked them into adjoining rooms, and when they were alone, the porter gone, he opened the connecting door and said quietly, 'I need to make a phone call—can you see to Ammy?'

'Yes, of course,' she murmured without looking at him, and a few minutes later, his call presumably made, he came to lean against the wall, watching while she tucked his daughter gently into bed. She didn't know if the tension was real or imagined. Didn't know if he felt as she felt—and didn't dare look at him to find out. She felt clumsy, inarticulate, and terrified of making a fool of herself. Of being rejected.

CHAPTER FIVE

'I'LL sit with her till she falls asleep,' Joel said quietly. 'Go and have your shower.'

'Yes,' Davina agreed jerkily. Hastily escaping, she collected up her nightwear from her case, scuttled past him and into the bathroom that joined the two rooms. Closing the door, she leaned back against it. She was shaking. And if he did—want her, take her, would he know? Be able to tell that no man had touched her since...? Swallowing hard, she wrenched on the shower, quickly undressed. Don't be a fool, Davina, of course he wouldn't be able to tell, she told herself. But it's been such a long time, you'd probably be... Stop it, Davina! You don't even know what he wants! But if he did... Frantically soaping herself, she rinsed, carefully dried, remembered her perfume was still in the bedroom, hunted feverishly among the sachets left for hotel guests, found body lotion, hand cream and massaged it into her body. Just in case. So stupid to be nervous—no, not nervous, terrified. Staring at herself in the misted mirror, she took deep breaths, tried to calm herself—and if she spent much longer in the bathroom he'd wonder what on earth she was doing, wouldn't he? Would probably knock, ask if she was all right—and she wasn't. She thought she felt sick—and she'd left her toothbrush in the bedroom.

Without giving herself time to think, she dragged on her pyjamas, wrenched open the bathroom door, saw on the periphery of her vision that he was sitting in the armchair beside the bed, beside a sleeping Ammy, muttered, 'Toothbrush,' grabbed her toilet bag, and dashed back into the bathroom. Would he understand she was nervous? she wondered as she scrubbed her teeth. But why should he? She was twenty-seven, hardly a child to be cosseted, and he thought she was experienced, thought there'd been other men. Her toothbrush gripped hard in her hand, her forearms along the white porcelain of the basin, she dragged a deep breath into her lungs, forced herself to stop acting like a twelve-year-old, and slowly straightened. Jamming the toothbrush into the glass, she carefully screwed the top back on the toothpaste, took one last deep breath, and walked out.

'All yours,' she announced, with only the slightest shake in her voice.

He nodded, got to his feet, and walked, slowly, into the bathroom. He left the door ajar. To prove that he wasn't nervous? She heard the rustle as he removed his clothing, the soft curse as he maybe jarred his bad arm, the rush of water as the shower was turned on, the sound of splashing—and then the shower was turned off, and she stiffened, her ears tuned to every sound. She heard the basin being filled with water, the soft sound of him shaving, a somehow intimate sound, and even though she'd been listening for him she still jumped like a scalded cat when he walked softly up behind her, turned her, tugged her into the adjoining room. He was stark naked.

'Joel . . .'

'Shh.' He moved behind her, moved her hair away from her nape, softly nuzzled her neck. 'I don't possess pyjamas,' he whispered against her skin, and his voice sounded deeper, rough, 'and even if I did it seemed rather a waste of effort to climb into them when I was only intending to remove them.' And as he spoke his hands

were busy with the buttons on the front of hers, slowly
sliding each one free until he could part the material,
and she sucked her breath in hard when he found the
warm, heavy swell of her breasts with his palms. She
could feel the small tremors that shook him, and that
was somehow comforting.

'Mind your bad shoulder,' she said thickly, stupidly.
'I will.'
And then she gasped as his hands slid slowly down-
wards, encountered the elastic of her waistband, hooked
his thumbs inside. His mouth still traced lazy patterns
on her nape, and she closed her eyes, obediently stepping
out of her pyjama bottoms as they whispered to her feet.

'Relax,' he urged, but she couldn't; she had to hold
herself together as warm palms briefly held her hips,
thumbs extended towards the back, pressed either side
of her spine, traced each vertebra as he reached her waist,
her ribs, and back to her breasts. His mouth moved to
her shoulder, trailed a line of fire as his lower body
touched yet more intimately against hers.

'Joel...'
He groaned, spun her to face him, found her mouth
with his, began to kiss her as though he would never
stop. Urgent, wild kisses that excited her, hurt her lungs
as she kissed him back as though he were the well of
life.

Clasping him close, her fingers dug into the strong
muscles of his back, roved almost feverishly across his
heated skin, until finally, finally, he took a deep breath,
eased her free, stared at her, his blue eyes almost black.

'Remember?' he demanded huskily.
'Yes.'
'And all this time I've dreamed of this. Needing,
wanting, yearning. And now I want to bury myself in

you, trap you in my arms, in my bed. So much—passion. Does it frighten you, Davina?' he asked thickly.

She swallowed hard, shook her head, but it did; it frightened her rigid.

'It frightens me,' he confessed. 'And do you have any idea how hard it was to sit beside you all day? Not touching, barely talking, when I wanted so much to reach for your hand, place it—here,' he said, his voice even thicker as he reached for it, placed it gently against his upper thigh. 'How much I wanted to reach out and un-button your shirt while you drove, trail my fingers—here.' Lifting his hand, he touched one finger to her throat, slid it down to the valley between her breasts. 'Wanted you to see me seeing you.'

With a little groan, she slid her arms round him, held him close.

'You said...'

'I lied.' Blue eyes speared and captured hers. 'It's been such a long, long time,' he murmured throatily.

'Yes.'

'And I want you every way there is for a man to want a woman.'

'Yes.'

'Is that what you want, Davina?'

'Yes.'

'Say it.'

Her voice barely audible, still choked, thick, she whis-pered, 'I want you.'

'Are you taking precautions?' he asked softly, gently.

'Yes.' This time she was. This time there would be no—complications, and her eyes misted for a moment in remembered anguish, a small barrier he would never be able to cross, because he did not know that the body he was loving had once been carrying his child.

'Vina?' he whispered in concern.

'It's all right,' she managed huskily. It's all right, an inner voice confirmed.

He gave a slow, gentle smile that was almost her un-doing, and then continued thickly, 'I have dreamed of this—oh, Davina, how I have dreamed of this. Such a beautiful lady and I want to hold you as you deserve, love you as you deserve...'

There was no pain, no discomfort, only pleasure given and received. A warm, pleasurable joining, dream-like, special, and as he rolled to cover her she touched her mouth to his strong throat, closed her eyes the better to savour something so long denied, held him tight, matched him movement for movement, pushed his chest away from hers so that she could see his face and, de-spite the long, angry graze, could admire the perfection of it, the beautiful blue of eyes drugged with passion, the sensuous curve of a mouth still waiting to claim hers, knowing that he timed himself to her, a gift freely given and received—and only then did she relax her arms so that he might claim her mouth with urgent finality, her secret still safe that he was the only man ever to have touched her so. That she had ever touched in such in-timacy. And now that it was a part of her again she didn't ever want to let it go.

He was not selfish in his giving, did not immediately roll away, expect it to be over, but moved to her side, curved her against him with his good arm, rested the bad across her waist, smiled into her eyes. 'Thank you.'

She gave a faint smile in return, loving the feel of his warmth against her, the weight of his arm, touched a gentle finger to his long eyelashes.

'Girl's lashes,' he mocked with teasing self-denigration.

'Mmm, but not wasted.'

'No, not if they can be enjoyed by you.'

And how many others? she wondered sadly.

'A fight worth losing, Davina?'

'Yes,' she agreed with a funny little sigh.

'Inevitable.'

Yes, she supposed it was. 'You really are separated from Celia?' she blurted.

'Yes.'

She nodded. Belief had to start somewhere.

'Tired?'

'Mmm.'

'Then ease up, burrow under the duvet, and sleep in my arms. Arm,' he corrected humorously.

Doing as he said, she wriggled into a more comfortable position, pressed a soft, almost shy kiss to his mouth, and closed her eyes. She woke in the night to his gentle touch, and sleepily, dreamily, touched him in return until both were aroused, and this time he took control, excited her, pleasured her, found zones she hadn't known existed that aroused her beyond belief, until she felt mindless with wanting, desperate for fulfilment, a rag doll with an aching core. He did not enter her until he had brought her to peak after peak of pleasure, and when she was almost ready to sob with frustration he whispered thickly, 'Beg.'

Shocked, but not unwilling, she whispered unevenly, 'Please, oh, please.' And he wrenched the moon out of orbit.

Turning, she sleepily surveyed him. I love you, she told him silently. I think I have always loved you. Even before we ever met, I think I loved you. Lids weighted, she drifted back to sleep and did not wake again until the sun sent a probe through the chink in the curtains, bathing her face in warmth. Joel was standing by the window, fully dressed; there was a faint smile on his face as he stood, arms folded, watching her.

'And before you ask,' he said softly, 'why I am standing over here, and you are over there, look beside you.'

Turning her head, she saw Ammy fast asleep where Joel had lain such a short time before.

'When...?' she began.

'At six. She must have heard me get up. Said she was lonely. Climbed in with you, and went back to sleep.'

'I never heard her... Why did you get up at six?'

'Because, my dear Davina,' he said softly, 'in sleep, you expand. By five-thirty I was clinging on to the edge of the mattress like a mountaineer without his crampons. I then received a kick. At that point, I gave up.'

'You should have woken me,' she murmured, able to tease now, provoke.

'I was going to. Get out my side, get in yours, only madam beat me to it.'

A smile in her eyes, she glanced at Ammy, then asked quietly, 'Joel, would it...? I mean, wouldn't she find it a bit odd, upsetting, finding her daddy in bed with someone who wasn't her mother?'

'I don't know,' he answered thoughtfully as his eyes too rested on his sleeping daughter. 'The situation has never arisen before—and don't look at me with those big disbelieving eyes; it hasn't. But that was partly why I got dressed, just in case. It's something we'll have to think about.'

'Yes.' Which sounded as though he was intending their—liaison to last a little bit longer, didn't it?

And then he smiled. 'It wasn't something I'd have needed to think about, of course, if my plans hadn't gone sadly awry.'

Puzzled, she asked, 'What does that mean?'

He shook his head. 'It doesn't matter, but I *will* have a word with Celia about it when I see her.'

Celia? Ask his ex-wife about making love to another woman? A shaft of pure jealousy pierced Davina. Celia had once lain like this. Celia had been loved by him, had loved him in return. Conceived his child. And he didn't seem to think it odd, or insensitive, to mention it. Shove it away, Davina. It's over, done, this is now, but the thought of him asking Celia about her continued to trouble her, put a little black cloud on the immediate horizon. 'What time is it?'

'Eight.'

'Eight?' she shrieked, then caught herself, and whispered urgently, 'But the ferry goes in half an hour!'

'Should go,' he agreed lazily. 'Would normally go.'

'But not today?'

'No, not today. Some hold-up the other end, not expected in until ten.'

With a sigh of relief, she sank back down. 'Time to have breakfast.'

'Yes.'

She looked at him. He looked back. Smiled.

'Pyjama jacket?' she prompted.

His smile widened. He walked to where it still lay on the floor, picked it up, held it on one finger. Waited.

'Please.'

He shook his head, joggled it to and fro. 'Come and get it.'

'I haven't got anything on!'

'I know.'

'Joel,' she protested, embarrassed.

He shook his head again. 'I'm immune to pleas. And if I can't make love to you as I would like, then I can at least—see you.'

Feeling stupid, she eased herself free, hurried towards him, and made a grab for the jacket. He held it out of her reach and with his free arm caught her against him.

'Good morning,' he greeted softly, his mouth only a fraction away from her own.

'Good morning,' she whispered, her voice a husky murmur, and to her surprise found that she was aroused. Felt full, and warm, and wanting. Sliding her arms round his neck, careful of his bad shoulder, she pushed her fingers into his thick hair at the nape, pressed her lower body against his.

'Not fair,' he murmured throatily.

'No.'

'And, much as I love her, I shall be extremely glad when I can hand Moppet over to her mother and have you all to myself. We could have made love this morning, lazily, beautifully—erotically. We could have showered together, soaped each other, played—games.'

With a little groan, she pressed herself closer, gently took his lower lip between her teeth, worried at it, soothed it with her tongue. In turn, he draped her pyjama-top round her shoulders, slid his hands beneath it—and did a bit of worrying of his own, until their breathing was laboured, until wanting each other's fulfilment was a deep ache.

Edging her towards the bathroom, towards privacy, he halted, groaned, gave a little grunt of laughter when his daughter's clear voice floated after them.

'Daddy? Ammy awake!'

He closed his eyes briefly, pressed a swift kiss to her nose, and murmured, 'Absolutely no sense of timing.'

Davina smiled, gave him a little push, and went to have her shower.

When they'd breakfasted and packed their belongings, they drove the short distance to the port. There was still no sign of the ferry, but it *would* come, they were assured, so Joel made the booking, and then another phone call, to whom Davina had no idea, because when she asked he merely smiled and touched a finger to her nose, and as they emerged from the terminal someone shrieked his name.

Turning, they both watched a tall, slim redhead hurry towards them—him, Davina mentally qualified, towards him. She was laughing as she hurled herself into his arms, pressed kisses to his mouth. He held her off, looked aloof, as uninterested as only he could look. And she gave an embarrassed smile and stepped back.

'Waiting for the ferry?' she asked foolishly, and Davina felt a momentary pang of sympathy for her.

He gave a little inclination of his head, even more distant if that was possible. 'Excuse me,' he added, punctiliously polite.

She gave a nervous giggle. 'We aren't going to wait. We're going on to Le Havre.'

'Good.'

Her smile even more fleeting, she turned away, hurried towards her companions, who were sitting in a green sports car, and Davina imagined her muttering, Let's get the hell out of here. Or had she pretended, for pride's sake, that Joel had been pleased to see her?

He turned his head, looked at Davina, one eyebrow raised. Lipstick didn't just graze his mouth; it positively plastered it. She didn't say a word. She didn't need to.

'Jealous?' he asked softly.

'No,' she refuted stonily, and the rat actually laughed.

'An old friend,' he murmured with wicked enjoyment. 'Presumably,' he tacked on.

'So I see.' She took a clean tissue from her pocket and handed it over.

'Thank you,' he said mockingly. 'Mirror?'

She silently took a tiny one from her bag, watched while he slowly removed all traces of lipstick.

'Better?'

She took the mirror, put it in her bag, slung her bag over her shoulder and began to walk off. 'A warning for me in that, was there? An example of how you treat ex-lovers?'

'No. And your insecurities are showing,' he murmured as he began to follow. 'The truth of the matter is, I haven't the faintest idea who she was. Someone I met briefly at a function, maybe.'

'And you don't like importuning women,' she stated.

'No.'

'Like to do your own running, in fact.'

'Yes, Davina, I like to do my own running. As I did—with you. And don't put labels on me.' Catching her unresponsive hand in his, Ammy on her other side, he led them down to the town. And slowly, slowly, as they wandered round the shops, she began to swallow her annoyance. An annoyance that was stupid and irrational. As he'd said, her insecurity. He must know hundreds of people, and if she was going to over-react every time he met someone she'd end up a neurotic.

'Better?' he asked gently, and she nodded. 'I really *don't* remember who she is,' he added wryly.

And that was supposed to comfort her? 'So many, are there?' she asked sweetly.

'Mmm,' he chuckled, 'hordes. And if you're expecting justification you won't get it. Come on.' Tugging her into a nearby shop, he bought her a bottle of expensive perfume. For being a good girl? Not causing a scene? And she hadn't expected justification. She didn't expect anything. He then bought Ammy a pretty ribbon for her hair and gently, carefully gave her a little ponytail, smiled at her, and lifted her so that she could admire it in one of the mirrors.

'Pretty,' she nodded, then beamed at her reflection.

'What do you say?' he asked as he put her down.

'Thank you,' she said obediently, with another little nod.

He glanced sideways at Davina, waited, and she gave a chagrined little grin.

'Thank you,' she said softly, and he smiled, a smile to curl her toes. And then he laughed, chuckled infectiously, but wouldn't tell her why.

Strolling hand in hand in the May sunshine, Ammy admiring herself and her new ribbon in the shop windows, Davina finally abandoned her pretence at stiffness. The truth of the matter was that whatever he did, said, was it didn't make a bit of difference to the way she felt about him, and suddenly, admitting that, instead of duller, everything looked brighter, the sky bluer, the sun warmer, and she wanted to tell him, let the words tumble over themselves—only it was too soon for that, wasn't it? And they might not be words he wanted to hear. Might never be words he wanted to hear.

They returned to the ferry terminal to find that there was still no ferry, and sat on the terrace to have lunch, await news. Leaving Ammy in the care of her father, she went to buy a book to read on the boat, a story-book for Ammy, and when she returned found him lying back in his chair, eyes closed, face tilted to the warm sun. Ammy was digging happily in a flowerbed.

'Joel,' she protested in humorous exasperation, 'she's eating mud!'

He opened one eye, regarded his daughter, and reproved half-heartedly, 'Ammy, don't eat mud.'

'Well, that's really likely to deter her, isn't it?'

'She's all right.'

'But she's getting filthy!'

'It'll wash off. Any news?'

'No.'

'We could have driven down to Le Havre, got the ferry from there, but . . .'

She blinked, remembered the redhead, and said nicely, 'No, thank you. I really don't mind waiting.'

He looked blank for a minute, and then he chuckled. 'Ah.'

'Quite.' Resuming her seat, she ordered another coffee. Anyway, redhead or no redhead, she felt as lazy as Joel appeared. It was nice just doing nothing. Watching him, the half-smile that still tugged at his mouth, the long lashes that once more hid his eyes, she sighed. She wasn't jealous, of course she wasn't; that was silly. Turning her attention to Ammy, she smiled when she stood up, brushed off her hands and came to lean against her father's knee.

'Swings.'

'Aren't any.'

'Are.'

He opened one eye, regarded her solemnly for a long moment, then followed her pointing finger towards a small fairground down on the beach.

'Swings.'

He groaned. 'What deplorable taste you have, Moppet.'

'I'll take her if you like,' Davina offered.

The eye swivelled in her direction. 'Someone else with deplorable taste?'

She laughed, accepted the handful of loose change he dug out of his pocket and, taking Ammy by the hand, led her towards the small fairground, and perhaps she did have deplorable taste, because she enjoyed it as much as Ammy—even if half her mind was on a lady with red hair whom he said he didn't remember. Had she once travelled with Joel? Taken care of his daughter? Or was it as he'd said—they'd briefly met at some function? Walked home together in the cold night air? Oh, shut up, Davina, she told herself. Insecurity is boring. But would the day come when he didn't remember who she was?

When she finally saw the ferry come over the horizon, she gave a sigh of relief, and even though she knew it would be another hour or so before it was turned around and they could board she persuaded Ammy that they needed to go back.

Joel was as they had left him, head back, face tilted to the sun, and she watched him for a moment unobserved, a faint shadow in her eyes. How long would it last? Weeks? Months? And when it ended would she really think it had been worth it? Please, God, she prayed. Ammy, not quite so besotted, or not in the same way, and with none of Davina's misgivings, launched herself on him with a little giggle. With a grunt, he opened his eyes and gave her a look of ill-usage, which she ignored, and began to explain the finer points of roundabouting.

'I'm going to tidy myself,' Davina murmured. Collecting her bag, she went to find the powder-room and give herself a little talking-to, and as she walked back to their table she glanced at other men. Men with families, men on their own, and not one of them could hold a candle to Joel. He looked—different. Special. Or had, she thought wryly when she found that both he and Ammy had disappeared. Puzzled, she stared around her, and when she still couldn't spot them gave an exasperated grunt. More roundabouting? she wondered. Or another old friend spotted? And why did men always disappear five minutes before you were due to be somewhere else? People were beginning to filter back to their cars, drive slowly into the inner car park, and she chewed worriedly on her lower lip. She liked everything *planned*. Knew she was a martyr to time, that she always arrived early everywhere, but she couldn't help it. That was the way she was. Always first in any queue going, and although logic told her there was plenty of time before they actually boarded that didn't give her any comfort.

'Over there.'

Turning in surprise, she saw that the lady at the next table was smiling at her and pointing towards the hotel they'd left only a few hours earlier.

'He took the little girl over there.'

'Over there?' Davina repeated blankly. 'What on earth for? Sorry,' she apologised lamely as she realised that the woman couldn't possibly know any more than she did because Joel was *not* the sort of man to impart information to anyone. 'Thanks.' Yanking her bag more firmly on to her shoulder, pushing her dark glasses on to her nose, she hurried across to the hotel. Perhaps he'd forgotten something—or Ammy had.

An elderly woman was at the desk, not the one who'd been there when they'd booked out, which was unfortunate. Walking across, Davina smiled weakly. '*Parlez vous anglais*?'

'*Oui*. 'Ow can I 'elp?'

'We booked out earlier, and——' Breaking off, deciding it was too complicated to explain, and feeling unutterably foolish, she murmured, 'I believe a tall, dark-haired man and a little girl came in?'

'Room fourteen, top of the stairs.'

'Room fourteen?' she queried, puzzled—they hadn't been in room fourteen. They'd been in twenty-three and twenty-four.

'*Oui.*' With Gallic indifference to the whims of tourists she pointed, and with a confused frown Davina walked in the direction indicated. Why on earth had Joel taken another hotel room? Especially with the ferry just in. And why not leave her a note? Tell her where he'd gone? She really did find people incomprehensible at times!

The door to room fourteen was ajar, and she halted uncertainly when she heard voices.

'You're a fool! Don't you ever learn?' a woman demanded angrily.

'Obviously not!' Joel denied shortly.

'And what's Helen going to say?'

'I don't give a damn what Helen is going to say!'

'Well, I do! You knew what she wanted, but would you agree? Oh, no, the great Joel Gilman thought he knew best!'

'I do know be——'

'Shut up! She's going to be *furious*!'

'It happened! I didn't damned well plan it!'

'Oh, that's really likely to appease her, isn't it? Well, what was she like? Pretty? Yes, of course she was pretty,' she muttered, sounding almost disgusted. 'They always are, aren't they?'

'Naturally,' he agreed pithily, 'and does it really matter?'

'No, and stop trying to put your shirt back on when I'm trying to take it off! I don't know why I put up with you, Joel, I really don't. One can only hope she knew *something* of what she was doing!'

Davina heard him sigh, heard the sound of bedsprings. 'She was—adequate, and at least her hands were soft!'

'Mine don't need to be soft! And why in God's name you have to choose innocents... Surely you could have found someone more experienced? And why, for once in your life, can't you just *think*?'

Innocent? Inexperienced? Suspicion only hovering in her mind, she slowly pushed the door wide. Joel was lounging on the bed, his shirt unbuttoned, pushed off one shoulder, and a blonde woman, dressed only in a small towel, was leaning over him—and suspicion crystallised into fact. They'd been discussing *her*, as though she were—irrelevant.

Whether they felt the draught from the open door or heard her shocked gasp Davina didn't know, only knew that they both turned to face her. They looked—guilty. *Déjà vu.* The two on the bed could have been Paul and Jenny; certainly it was as though time had travelled backwards; perhaps she even said the same words.

'Having a nice time, are we?'

'Wonderful,' he affirmed sarcastically, 'and don't jump to conclusions.'

'No,' Davina agreed woodenly, 'certainly I wasn't the one doing any jumping. Caen,' she murmured bitterly. 'Had to be Caen, didn't it?'

'Davina...' he began warningly.

'Remember this one, do you? And what do I get this time? Jewellery? Or is it always perfume?' she asked harshly. 'Have a woman in every port? Except Dieppe, of course. Dieppe was a definite no-no. And I bet *she* isn't inexperienced. I bet she's a real wow between the sheets!'

There was a gasp. 'Now wait just a minute,' the blonde began furiously. 'I——'

'No, you wait,' Davina insisted as she took a step into the room, so blazingly angry, so hurt and humiliated that she didn't even stop to think what she was saying! 'I'm the dummy here, and I'll say what I please! Not even a note!' she castigated Joel. 'A quick tumble, was it, and back before I missed you?'

'Don't be cru——'

'Crude?' she demanded. 'Me?' Turning her attention to the woman once more—older than Davina had first thought, she decided almost dispassionately, early thirties maybe, and most *certainly* experienced—and because her mouth nearly always ran faster than her brain when she was upset, and because she felt so unbelievably betrayed, so—lost she choked, 'I hope *you* know the rules, because I didn't even get to see the manual, but then I would guess you aren't merely—adequate, are you?'

'Don't be absurd. This is——'

'I don't care who it is!' she yelled. 'I certainly don't want to know her name! And where's poor little Ammy while this speedy seduction is going on? Assuming it is speedy and that you *were* intending to catch the ferry!'

'Davina——'

'You *did* deliberately pursue me! Seduce me! Just to see if you could, didn't you? And I made it so *easy*, didn't I?'

Struggling to his feet, his face grim, he hitched his shirt back on to his shoulder and took a step towards her. 'You really believe that, do you?'

'Yes, I really believe that! What else am I supposed to believe when I find my...'

'Lover?' he asked nastily.

'Companion,' she gritted, 'wrapped in the arms of another woman the minute my back's turned?'

'Well, I imagine you might believe it was perfectly innocent,' he proposed in a slow drawl that was far more cutting than anger would have been.

'Oh, do you? But then it presumably doesn't happen to you, does it?'

'N——'

'But it happens to me, doesn't it? A fact you know very well!'

'Davina——'

'Don't Davina me, you b——! And don't, please, tell me you just bumped into her in the corridor!'

'I wasn't going to. And if we're levelling accusations, what about poor Michael?'

'We'll leave Michael out of this, thank you! And you *knew* I was engaged, yet still pursued me!'

'Did I? And you were so very unwilling to be caught, were you?'

Remembering her behaviour, she glared at him. 'I didn't say that! But your actions have hardly been those of a gentleman, have they? You deliberately ignored——'

'Because I thought you'd made him up!' he said savagely.

'Well, I didn't!'

'Then that makes you a cheat. Or is that what this is all about, Davina? Still punishing me?'

'Of course, what else did you expect? Betrayed women carry the betrayal for life! Didn't you know that, Joel?'

'No. And what was I? A one-night stand?'

'Why not? It surely didn't mean any more to you if you can rush off the moment you're alone and into the arms of another woman. Just pick her up, did you? A random snatch?'

'No,' he denied tightly.

'Oh, an assignation!' she retorted with vicious admiration.

He looked for a moment as though he might hit her, and then that awful derision settled on his face. He even managed a cynical smile. Taking another step forward, he pushed her out into the corridor and closed the door behind him. 'You want to fight? Then we'll fight. But not in front of—witnesses! Now, you want to hear my side of it?'

'No.'

'You want to believe your own sordid little truths?'

'*Mine*?' she choked. '*Mine*? Dear God, but you're unbelievable! You were on the *bed* with her! Half-naked! And if I'd come just ten minutes later...'

'You'd have seen nothing! And Michael? He exists?'

'Of course he exists!'

'I see. Exists to be punished.'

'Naturally! You said it yourself, Joel! Men are there to be used.'

He gave a bitter little laugh. 'And I thought all that reluctance was because of nerves.'

'Did you? How quaint, when the truth was so much simpler—I was forcing myself to respond. I do hope you enjoyed it!'

'Oh, I did. One could definitely say that I enjoyed it,' he agreed acidly. 'Goodbye, Davina. Have a really good life.' His face set and totally devoid of expression, he opened the door, walked inside and closed it in her face.

Her lower lip trembling, her eyes full of tears, she aimed a vicious kick at the door. 'Liar,' she whispered. 'Defiler.' Her chest rising and falling as she tried to keep air in her lungs, her face taut and aching, she swung away, leaned against the wall beside the door, stared blindly at the flock wallpaper. Why had he done it? Because it was only a game? To chase and discard? Pay her back for what she had once done to him? Said to him? But you didn't have to say that, Davina, about men... With a little sob, she turned to stumble down the stairs—and saw a plump, brown-haired man climbing towards her, Ammy in tow. She held a bunch of wild flowers clasped in one tiny hand. Beaming, she exclaimed happily, 'Look, Vina, I picked some flowers for Mummy!'

Mummy? *Mummy*? The man gave her a searching glance, looked as though he was about to speak, then obviously thought better of it. He gave her a vague smile, and opened the bedroom door. Ammy rushed inside, eager to offer her gift.

'Look, Mummy! Flowers!'

Mummy. Not a mistress, not someone he'd just picked up, but Celia, his ex-wife. And she'd just said... accused... Oh, Davina. Her face distraught, she stumbled back to the door, stared inside. Celia was perched on the bed, Ammy on her knee. The brown-haired man was smiling at them, and Joel had his back to them all, staring from the window.

Celia looked up, gave Davina a cold look, and said quietly, 'Joel.' He turned and stared at Davina with utter indifference.

'I... The ferry's in,' she blurted stupidly.

'Is it? How very kind of you to let me know,' he murmured derisively. 'Best go and catch it, then, hadn't you? And Davina,' he added, as though she were about to leave, 'when you remove your suitcase, leave the car keys in the boot, will you? Unlocked, of course.' Turning away, he resumed his contemplation of the scene outside.

'But I . . .'

'Goodbye, Davina. George, close the door.'

George looked indecisive, glanced quickly away from Davina's hurt eyes. Celia ignored her.

Backing out, Davina closed the door herself. Down the stairs, past the woman at the desk, she walked blindly out into the sunshine. Crossing the busy road without even looking, she unlocked the boot, removed her suitcase, and laid the keys gently inside before closing it.

CHAPTER SIX

HE'D catch her up, of course he would. It couldn't end like this. He'd apologise, she would... They'd both said things in anger... Shaking so much that she could barely see straight, Davina walked into the terminal, found a seat beside the plate-glass window, stared without seeing at the rows of cars waiting to board, and wondered at her behaviour. Where had all those words come from? About hating men? It couldn't only be put down to pride. They'd welled up as though they'd been dammed up inside her for years. She didn't hate men. Paul hadn't ruined her life; on the contrary, because of what had happened, she'd made a success of it. So why had she said them? Because subconsciously they were true? No! They weren't. Of course they weren't. She'd avoided emotional entanglements with men because she hadn't wanted to be hurt, not because she hated them.

With a funny little whimper, she put her hands over her eyes, then realised how she must look, the impression she would be giving, and the last thing she wanted was for someone to come up and ask her if she was all right. Gulping in a deep breath, she removed her hands, clenched them in her lap instead, and continued to stare at the cars, at the ferry—the *Normandie*, blue and white, lifeboats slung from their davits... Don't think, Davina, she told herself. It'll be all right. He'll understand when he's calmed down that the words were said out of anger, hurt.

'Don't jump to conclusions', he'd said, but she had, shoving both feet into her mouth at the same time. And she'd said... Swallowing hard, she stared grimly at her hands, picked agitatedly at a nail. But why had Celia been wearing a towel? Why had Joel's shirt been undone? Perhaps... Why can't you ever think first, Davina? Why do you have to say things that can't be retracted? But if they hadn't been talking about her, who had they been talking about? Adequate. Inexperienced. And it hurt so much. Remembering their lovemaking, the sheer innovation of it, she felt doubly wretched. And how could she have told him that she'd forced herself to respond? How *could* she? Had he believed her? No, of course he hadn't, wouldn't, nor about Michael... With a long shudder, she returned her attention to the scene outside. Was this how she'd felt when she'd seen Paul with Jenny? She couldn't remember. Yes, she could. Numb, that was how she'd felt. At first, anyway. Later there had been anger, when Paul had come to see her, explain. *Explain*, she thought with a bitter laugh. Would Joel come? No, Joel wasn't like Paul. Perhaps she could write to him, explain... But who was Helen?

The Tannoy flared into life, making her jump, and, barely aware of what she was doing, she joined the queue of weary passengers, trudged slowly forward, but it worried her, nagged at her, the thought of someone called Helen. Halting, unaware of the confusion behind her as the rest of the queue stumbled to a ragged halt, she tried to recall any mention of a Helen before. In Andorra, or at the first hotel... 'What?'

'Ticket,' the official repeated patiently.

'Ticket?'

He gave an exasperated sigh. 'Yes. Ticket. Where is it?'

Staring at him, she confessed miserably, 'In the car.'

'Then go and *get* in the car.'

'No, I can't, I . . .'

'Madam,' he began again, even more patiently, 'either go and get your ticket or get in the car. You're holding everyone up.'

Glancing round, suddenly embarrassed, but beginning to be angry too at her weak-willed behaviour, she hurried across to the desk, asked for a ticket in a voice that sounded gritted, paid for it with her credit card, and hurried back to the dwindling queue. Thrusting the ticket at the official, her eyes daring him to make any further comment, she stood silently fuming while he carefully scrutinised it—and saw Joel's car edge on to the end of the row nearest her. Snapping her head away from him, she grabbed back her ticket and hurried on to the ferry. And if he could drive into the loading area, he could have driven through France. So why hadn't he? Because he liked to pursue lone females? Was that why he'd been so angry? Not explained? Because half of her accusations had hit the mark? And now she came to think about it, couldn't some of the things he'd said over the past few days that on the surface had been kind, comforting have a different interpretation? Hadn't there sometimes been a rather calculating light in his eye? As though he was testing her? Gauging her response?

Riven by doubt, she hurried up on to the deck. Dumping her case at her feet, she leaned her arms along the rail and stared with unseeing eyes at the rows of houses, hotels, the small fun-fair where such a short time ago she had laughed with Ammy . . . You should have listened . . . What was there to hear? Excuses? Lies? Not necessarily; there might have been a very good reason for his shirt to have been half off his shoulder. He wouldn't have been...not when Ammy was around—and George, she suddenly remembered. Who *was* George? Celia's new partner?

There was a rumble beneath her feet, the clank and rattle of chains being loosed, the car deck being made secure, and then they were going into reverse, throwing up a wake as the distance between ship and shore slowly widened. Staring towards the small hotel where a dream had died, she tried to see if an attractive blonde woman had come out, was watching, as she was watching. Whether she held a little dark-haired girl by the hand.

If she'd had time to think...not come upon them so suddenly... Was that who he'd been making all those phone calls to? Celia? Arranging to meet, leave Ammy with her? Perhaps they weren't really separated; perhaps he'd lied. Probably they had separate holidays. Perhaps it was one of those new-fangled modern marriages where they each did their own thing. She could go and seek him out on the ferry, ask—if he didn't seek her out. But he wouldn't; she knew he wouldn't. And she wished to God she had never met him again. And if she'd thought about it, maybe she would have hoped that anyone seeing her would think the wind caused the tears in her eyes, the sting of the spray, but she didn't think about it, and when she was tired of standing she found a seat inside, huddled miserably in it and waited for the hours to pass. Twice she went to see if she could find him, a half-formed idea in her bewildered mind that they would talk, explain, but she couldn't find him, and so she drank endless cups of coffee that she didn't want, and stared at the empty sea. It had to have been the shortest romance on record. Romance? Was that what it was? Impatient with herself, angry with herself, she opened her book, stared unseeingly at the dancing print. *You* wanted it, Davina.

You could have said no. He didn't promise unending love. He didn't promise anything at all... Didn't have to *cheat*, though, did he?

It was dark when the ferry docked in Portsmouth, and if anyone had asked her what the crossing had been like she wouldn't have been able to tell them, although presumably she would have noticed if it had been rough. Humping her heavy case through the vast dock area and out to the road with the vague idea of finding a cab, she saw Joel. He was sitting in his car, watching her, and when she halted uncertainly he climbed out, walked round the car and held the passenger door open. He looked unbelievably grim.

'Get in.'

When she only continued to hover uncertainly, he wrenched her case out of her hand, and indicated with a jerk of his head for her to get in the passenger seat, and when she had done so he slung her case in the boot, and got behind the wheel. With his right hand, he reached across to knock the lever into drive, and pulled out on to the road.

'Joel...'

'Shut up. Don't talk, don't move—don't, in fact, do anything. I am really not in the mood.'

'Then why did you pick me up?'

'Because I'm a gentleman.'

'Huh!'

'Davina,' he warned ominously, 'be quiet.'

'I...'

He looked at her, and she shut up. For the moment. But her mind wasn't silent; it held long and grim conversations with him in her head, and if he was going to continue to treat her like a naughty child...

When he asked for directions to her house, she gave them, her voice tight, and then couldn't bear it any longer.

'Look, I'm sorry I jumped to conclusions.'

'Are you?'

'Yes. So can we either have a damned great row and get it over with or...?'

'Or?' he asked silkily.

'Or let me out and I'll get a train—or something.'

'The "something" presumably being hitch-hiking. Or were you intending to ring Michael?' he asked nastily.

'Michael doesn't exist,' she told him shortly. 'And don't talk to me as though I'm four.'

'Then why did you lie?'

'Because I was hurt, dammit! Turn left at the next junction, towards the Devil's Punchbowl, and then it's just up the lane on the right. If you'd explained...'

'You gave me a chance?' he demanded.

'Yes. No. Pull up in front of that——' Breaking off, she stared in bewilderment at the light spilling along her front path from the open door. 'Why is...?' she began, and then realisation hit her. 'Oh, my God. Don't say I've got burglars!' Before the car had even fully stopped, she was out of her door and hurrying towards her cottage.

'For heaven's sake!' Joel castigated angrily as he grabbed her, halted her forward flight. 'Don't you have *any* sense? You're really intending to go rushing into your house not knowing if there are burglars still inside?' Thrusting her behind him, he strode up the path, and then stopped as a bulky, fair-haired figure emerged. He looked at Joel and demanded aggrievedly, 'Who the devil are you?' then saw Davina and, thrusting Joel aside, marched up and grabbed her shoulders.

'Where the *hell* have you been?'

'Michael?' she queried weakly. 'What on earth are you doing here?'

'Looking for you! *Wednesday*, you said! You distinctly said Wednesday!'

'Yes, I know, but——'

'This is Friday! Friday!'

'I *know* it's Friday! But if——'

'I've been going out of my mind!' he continued angrily. 'Up here, down there, ringing God knows who, and I——'

'Michael!' she roared. 'Will you please just shut up?' When he subsided with a mutinous huff, she took a deep breath, and tried again. 'Look, this is... Joel? *Joel*!' Running down the path, she grabbed his arm just as he dumped her suitcase on the path and slammed down the boot lid.

'Doesn't exist?' he queried scathingly. 'Who's that, then? The spectre at the bloody feast?' Shrugging off her arm, he strode to his door, wrenched it open and climbed inside.

'But he's not... Joel, I can *explain*!'

'I'm sure you can.' Slamming his door, regardless of whether her fingers might have been in the way or not, he released the brake, rammed his foot on the accelerator and roared away.

Stamping her foot in frustration, she kicked aggravatedly at her suitcase. 'You brainless cretin! And if you can't listen, don't come back!'

'What the hell was that about? Who *was* that?'

'Joel,' she muttered as she continued to stare after the car.

'Nice chap,' he said sarcastically. 'Certainly his manners leave a lot to be desired.' Grabbing up her suitcase, he began to carry it up the path. 'Well, come on, Davina, don't just stand there! I want an explanation!'

Yeah, you and everyone else. 'And why are you wearing an overcoat? It's *summer*!' Ignoring his look of astonishment, she stalked into the cottage ahead of him. Probably his mother had told him never to cast a clout till May was out, and he'd taken the advice literally! And if Michael hadn't been there, would Joel have come in with her? To talk? Everyone seemed to have such lousy timing of late. Including herself.

When she'd explained, roughly, why she was late, she asked, 'So why were you looking for me? You weren't really worried, were you?'

'Of course I wasn't,' he denied impatiently and without any thought that he might be hurting her feelings. 'I wanted you for a talk at Claridge's. Tomorrow.'

'Tomorrow? I can't do tomorrow!'

'No choice; I've already agreed.'

'But I've only just got back!'

'I *know* that! But when I agreed you could do it I thought you would have two days to get yourself prepared, didn't I?'

'Yes,' she agreed with a sigh.

'I expect you're tired,' he observed, a clear understanding in his voice that *something* must account for her odd behaviour.

'Yes,' she agreed.

'Certainly you *look* terrible.'

'Thanks. What time do I have to be there?'

'Noon. You aren't *ill*, are you?' Michael wasn't very good with people being ill.

'No,' she denied wearily. 'Are you coming with me? To the talk?'

'Me? Why would I come? You know I hate that sort of thing.'

'Yes.'

A sudden look of suspicion on his ruddy face, as though this might be some new and disturbing trend, he asked worriedly, 'Then why did you ask?'

'I've no idea,' she confessed.

'You could come to the office first, if you like,' he offered, not very convincingly. 'I mean, if you need support or something. Although why you should I can't imagine. You never have before.'

'No, no, that's all right. Just the usual stuff, is it?'

'Yes, the front desk will tell you where to go.'

'Fine.'

He continued to watch her for a few minutes, then demanded, 'You sure you aren't ill?'

'Yes, Michael, I'm sure.'

'And you'll be all right for Wiltshire next week?'

'Yes. And Edinburgh.'

'Good, good. I'd better go, then, let you get some sleep.'

'Yes. I'll ring you after the talk.'

He nodded and, still looking perplexed, walked out to his car.

Poor Michael. Relationships defeated him. With a bitter laugh, she admitted that they defeated her too. Locking up, she made her way tiredly up to bed. Everything seemed unreal, as though it had never happened. But it surely couldn't end like this, in misunderstanding and bitterness. And if she went to see Joel? If she tried to explain, would he listen? And although she told herself to put it out of her mind, get some sleep she couldn't, but continued to gnaw at it like a mouldy bone. His behaviour, her behaviour... And when she woke in the morning she felt as muddled and confused as she had the day before, and every time the phone rang against all expected odds she somehow thought it would be him. Only it never was. And the need to know for *sure* was overtaking all other needs, and if he wouldn't get in touch with her, then she would have to get in touch with him. And if she had been wrong? What then? After all, she hadn't *expected* it to last, had she? Only there was this vision, of a future, with a child like Ammy, with dark hair and blue eyes, of a home, warmth, laughter—sharing.

She gave the talk at the hotel, with no clear idea of what she said, and the moment she could escape she drove to Ham Common where Joel lived, to the address that he'd written on the registration card in the hotel. Perhaps even then she'd known she would need to remember it. A different house from the one she'd gone to before, all those years ago. But the reason wasn't so different, was it? It was still because she wanted him.

Hands on the bars, she stared through the high railings at his car parked in a small forecourt overhung with trees and shrubs. Wisteria climbed across the front of the red-brick house, blossom scattered across the gravel drive like confetti. Taking a deep breath, she pushed open the gate, walked along the short drive, and rang the bell. She could hear it echoing inside the house like something from a movie. There was a little buzz, a click, and the door opened.

Surprised, not to say a little alarmed, she hesitantly pushed it wide and peeped inside, and then just stared because for some reason she had expected opulence—antiques maybe, plush carpets—but it seemed stark, functional, very modern. Black on white, white on black, fronds of greenery from large leafy plants in black marble pots. White walls, black-framed modern paintings. Joel's own? Peering at the signature on the nearest, she shook her head at a name she didn't know.

She should have come last night, when she'd had anger to sustain her, but a night's reflection had taken the anger away, leaving her feeling unsure, inadequate. Staring at the spiral staircase, black wrought iron, she called tentatively, 'Joel?'

'Up here.' His voice was cool, uninterested, and she nearly turned and ran away. Nearly. But she was used to wearing armour, used to projecting an image of control, cool professionalism, and so she took a deep breath, like a swimmer preparing to dive, and with a hand that felt damp, sweaty she grasped the rail and began to climb up, careful not to slip on the metal treads. As she turned the last curve, she halted, gasping in surprise. Colour, so much colour, a sunburst of warmth that came as such a contrast to the hall below. And space, so much space, all rooms knocked into one vast amphitheatre peopled with easels like a bizarre futuristic landscape. And at one end, beneath a glass dome, stood Joel. He was chewing on the end of a very long paintbrush and staring at a canvas propped before him. There was a small panel of switches on the wall beside him, one of them, presumably, to release the front door.

'You saw me arrive,' she stated softly.

'Yes. Make it short; I'm busy.'

She gave a weak, unamused laugh. Busy. So dismissive, when for the past hours she'd been filled with uncertainty, anguish. Staring at him, at black hair that tumbled across his brow, at an unshaven chin, an old workshirt that was daubed in paint, jeans and bare feet, she felt again that little lurch of her heart—and suppressed it. Wondered again at her foolishness in getting

involved with him. He wasn't for her. Men like Joel were
never for people like her, but neither was she a naughty
little girl to be dismissed so summarily. And even if they
never went anywhere from here, she needed to know the
truth, needed *him* to know the truth.

Walking slowly towards him, her low-heeled shoes
slapping on varnished floorboards, she began quietly,
'Michael is my editor.'

'Is he?' he asked indifferently.

'Yes, not my fiancé.'

He gave a mirthless smile, and then he did look at
her. A glance only, which took in the tailored skirt, the
cream silk shirt, and then he returned his attention to
his canvas. 'And it took you nearly all day to think up
the excuse, did it?'

'No,' she denied. Well, she'd known it wasn't going
to be easy. 'I had to give a talk. At Claridge's. That's
why Michael was waiting for me last night.'

'Is it?'

'Yes.' Look at me, she wanted to shout. Stop being
so controlled! But then he was controlled, she remembered. Arrogant. His energies channelled into one goal
at a time. And this time she wasn't the goal, and just
for a moment her composure slipped as she remembered
the way he had touched her, the feel of his kisses. 'Why
didn't you tell me that it was Celia?'

'Does it matter?'

'Yes, it matters,' she admitted in the same quiet voice.

'Why?'

'Because it does. You were on the bed together.'

'Mmm, she wanted to inspect my shoulder.'

'Why?'

He glanced at her, raising one eyebrow.
'Curiosity? Concern?'

'She was half-naked.'

'Yes, she'd just got out of the shower.'

Dragging in a deep breath, feeling helpless and irritated, she just stared at him. 'And that's it? End of explanation? I have to drag every scrap of information out of you? What was she *doing* there?'

'Waiting for me.'

'Why?'

'To collect Ammy.'

Yes, to collect Ammy. 'It was Celia you were phoning?'

'Correct.'

'But if the ferry had been on time,' she frowned, 'we would have been long gone.'

'Yes. How lucky it was late,' he drawled sarcastically. 'Finished?'

'No,' she replied impatiently. 'I need to understand. You insisted on going to Caen, not Dieppe, because you knew Celia would be there. Knew we would miss the late ferry...'

'No.'

'No? What do you mean, *no*?'

His attention fixed seemingly firmly on his canvas, he recited with scant patience, 'I knew Celia was holidaying further up the coast from Caen, and if for some reason we had to wait for a ferry, or just missed one, I was intending that we should drive up and drop Ammy off.'

'So why didn't we?'

'Because when I rang she wasn't there.'

'So you rang her again the next morning.'

'Yes. She was out playing golf, so I left a message to say that the ferry had been delayed and, if she could, to come to the hotel.'

'So we sat outside the ferry terminal so that you could watch for her.'

'Yes. She came straight off the course, grubby and irritable...'

'And decided to have a shower while you talked.'

'Yes.'

So simple? Really so simple? 'I see.'

'Good.'

Oh, Joel... 'You don't believe I lied, do you? About...'

'Forcing yourself? No.'

'Why? You must know...'

'That I'm attractive to women? Yes, I do.'

'Joel! It's not a game! If you'd explained ... If you'd cared for me, you'd have *made* me listen.'

'Would I? And by the same token if you'd cared, so would you.'

'I was angry, hurt, humiliated. *You* should have understood that. You knew what happened with Paul.'

'Mmm,' he agreed uninterestedly, his attention still fixed on his canvas. 'So I did. And is that what you did to him? Accused without knowing the facts? Assumed?'

'No. Paul was naked. So was Jenny. Wrapped in each other's arms. Caught in the act. Like some awful farce. And if I hadn't decided on the spur of the moment to go to the new flat to hang the curtains as a surprise for Paul... Well, it was a surprise all right,' she added bitterly. 'They were having a lovely time. He said it just happened, hadn't been planned or anything, as though that made it acceptable. Jenny had asked to see the new flat... But then Paul was supposed to be in love with me,' she finished sadly. 'I knew you weren't.'

'Did you? How perspicacious you are.'

Hurt, dying just a little bit more inside, she asked quietly, 'And I'm not to be forgiven, am I? For—assuming.'

'No.'

'Why?'

'Why?' His head on one side, he put the brush between his teeth and fractionally altered the position of the canvas. Then, removing the brush, he gave her an indifferent glance. 'Why do you think?'

'Because you never really wanted me? Because the chase was more exciting than the—capture?' He didn't answer, merely slanted her a glance of mock-interest. 'Because you're angry?' she persevered with ridiculous hope.

'Angry?' he queried with an amused quirk to his mouth. 'No, Davina, I'm not angry, I'm totally indifferent. Unlike you, I don't hold post-mortems, even mental ones. I made a mistake. So, apparently, did you.'

'Yes, but then I think I knew that all along,' she said quietly. 'And an apology isn't going to make any difference, is it?'

'No.'

Not even if she begged. And that she wouldn't do. 'It's funny, isn't it?' she asked reflectively. 'I didn't expect it to last. I didn't, in fact, expect *anything*. No self-worth, you see, and that's rather tragic, isn't it? Perhaps I should thank you because you have at least made me see that I'm worth more. A great deal more.'

'Then I'm glad to have been of service. Go back to Michael. He obviously doesn't mind being duped.'

'He isn't duped. I told you, he's my editor.'

'Fine. Do give him my regards. Did you tell him?'

'No.'

'Wise girl.'

'Yes,' she agreed rather sadly. 'Beginning to be, anyway. One more question. Who's Helen?'

'My physio. Goodbye, Davina.'

'Goodbye,' she whispered. Yet she stood for a little while longer, just staring at him. How long would it have lasted if she hadn't gone into that hotel in Caen? How long *could* it have lasted? Not long, she supposed sadly. There was no trust between them. No *knowledge*. 'How long would it have lasted, Joel?'

'Lasted? I wasn't intending for it to last at all.'

Wincing, she gave a funny little laugh. 'So if it hadn't ended in Caen it would have ended in Portsmouth, is that what you're saying?'

'Clever girl. There's something else?' he asked helpfully.

'No, nothing else. I——'

'Oh, goody, is it another row?' a saccharine voice asked from behind her.

Spinning round, she came face to face with a cool-looking Celia. 'No,' she denied awkwardly. 'I was just going. I didn't know,' she began quietly, muddled. 'He never said—that you were his ex-wife.'

'Ex-lover,' Joel corrected in the same uninterested drawl. 'In the interests of accuracy, Celia and I were never married. Were we, my dear?'

'No.'

A bewildered frown on her face, Davina turned to face Joel once more. 'But you said...' No, he hadn't. He'd said they should never have lived together, and she'd thought at the time that it was an odd way of putting it. Got it wrong all along the line, hadn't she? Returning her attention to Celia, she murmured stiltedly, 'I'm sorry I was rude to you in France.'

'Rude? You were viciously insulting!'

'I know. I'm sorry, I thought...'

'You made it very clear what you thought! However, being a magnanimous sort of person...'

Joel gave a derisive snort and she gave him a sweet smile. A key was dangling mockingly from one finger. 'You really are a rat, aren't you?' she asked him. 'Can't you see how much she's hurting?'

'Self-inflicted, dear lady, self-inflicted, and might one ask what you are doing here? Again.'

'Looking for George.'

'Ah. You should keep the leash a little shorter.'

'Bound up? Tagged? Monitored?'

'It might stop you keeping losing him.'

'The way it stopped you losing me?'

The brush snapped, a soft little crack that sounded loud in the large room, but his voice was unchanged, still smooth, still derisive. 'Go and be bitchy with someone else, Celia. And take Davina with you.'

She sighed. 'Can we start this conversation again? George was supposed to pick up that little line drawing. Did he?'

'No. I haven't seen him, I told you. He's probably on the golf course.'

'He'd better not be,' she said darkly. Glancing at her watch, she gave another impatient sigh. 'Where is it?'

Joel pointed his brush towards the corner and Celia walked across to collect a flat tissue-wrapped packaged. Gently unfolding it, she stared, gave a soft whistle. 'Oh, Joel, it's brilliant. When you do work like this, I could forgive you anything.'

He grunted.

She smiled and, walking back, took Davina's arm and urged her towards the stairs. 'We're disturbing his concentration. Come along. Time is money. Money is time.'

When they reached the hall, Celia's attention still focused on her package, the smile still on her mouth, she halted, stared at Davina, showed her the drawing. 'What do you think?'

Staring down at the line drawing of a naked young man, face turned towards the artist, a smile of pure mischief on his face, she said inadequately, 'It's beautiful.'

'Yes, and clever.'

'Joel did it?'

'Mmm. A commission—it's being picked up from the gallery this afternoon.'

'Your gallery?' she asked.

'Mmm, mine and George's.' Carefully folding the tissue back over the drawing, she asked, 'Want some advice? Forget him. Artists are hell to live with.'

As Celia would know. 'You don't live here?'

'Hell, no, we get on much better when there's a few miles between us.' A more friendly expression on her face, she asked curiously, 'You really want him?'

'Yes,' Davina admitted honestly. There was no point in lying.

'Then why on earth did you go out of your way to alienate him in France? Jump to so many conclusions?'

'Because it happened before.'

'With Joel?' she asked in obvious surprise.

'No, someone else. And because I don't know him very well, because . . .'

'You feel more for him than he feels for you?'

'Maybe.'

Celia shrugged. 'Men aren't worth the anguish,' she said dismissively.

'Not even George?'

'George?' she laughed. 'Good heavens, no! George is my partner. We run the gallery together—and he's teaching me to play golf, which is why we were in France, but anything else, no.'

Dismissing irrelevancies, Davina asked, 'Art gallery? You sell Joel's paintings?'

'Mmm, some of them anyway. Mostly he works from commission. You don't know much about him, do you?'

'No.'

'He's difficult, moody, clever... And you look as though you could use a drink,' Celia added with rather rough kindness. 'If we can't have his attention, we can at least drink his whisky.'

Davina didn't know why she followed her towards the lounge, perhaps because she felt incapable of making any more decisions.

'You shouldn't have come,' Celia advised as she picked up the decanter and held it out invitingly, and when Davina shrugged and nodded she poured them both a generous measure. 'He doesn't like being pursued, or pinned down—but then, if you hadn't, you wouldn't have discovered what a so-and-so he can be. He inspires hate, anger, exasperation—desire, and women have been bending their fingers on him for years. Too damned attractive for his own good.'

'Yes. Did you love him?'

'Love?' With a little shrug, Celia admitted, 'I don't know if I know what it is; all I do know is that we were never right for each other. I always liked my independence too much, expect people to fit in with my ideas, not the other way about, and Joel can be an awkward cuss. I had so many plans for him... Ah, well, water under the bridge. We'd already split up when I discovered I was pregnant. He has a very moral streak, you know,' she added, as though she somehow found the fact incomprehensible, 'and insisted we stay together for the baby's sake. And when she was born he seemed to think I should stay at home all the time and look after her. Don't get me wrong, I love that little mite dearly, would do anything for her, but I simply am not the mumsy type—and why I'm telling you all this I really don't know! I have to get back to the gallery.'

'A short leash,' Davina murmured, remembering something that had been said upstairs.

'What? Oh, yes, and no one but a fool would think that keeping me on a leash would work. Finished?'

Quickly swallowing the last of her drink, Davina handed the empty glass back. 'Give my love to Ammy.'

'Will do,' Celia murmured as she began to usher Davina out, 'and if I were you I'd find myself a nice career, tell him to go hang.'

'Yes,' she agreed tonelessly. It would be nice to be as positive as the other woman—as positive as she'd thought she was until Joel had erupted into her life again, and, because of that, she now wanted something more. Wanted Joel, who didn't want her, but, thanks to Celia, she was beginning to understand a little bit more about him, why he behaved as he did—for all the good that would do her.

Her fragile composure beginning to shatter, she quietly left, absently waving to Celia as the other woman got into her car. Opening her own car door, she climbed in and closed it quietly behind her. She didn't look back. He had given her something special—and then wrenched it cruelly away. She'd made a mistake—and that would not be forgiven. Her throat hurt, and her chest, but she would not cry. And when she was eighty, if she lived to be eighty, she would not regret it. But it was silly to fill your life with dreams, much better to be practical, which meant getting on with her own life. She had a talk to give in Wiltshire in a few days—perhaps she'd go early, have a good look round first. Then up to Edinburgh for more talks; she might even go out to see her parents. Keep busy, that was the thing. You're a fatalist, Davina, she told herself. Yes. Ever since Jenny and Paul, she'd been a fatalist. She would rail against it from time to time, but at the end of the day that was what it came right down to. Fatalism. She didn't know if that was a good thing or not but, whatever it was, it was damnably painful—and he wasn't worth her anguish, was he?

She gave her talk in Wiltshire, and then Edinburgh. It was unbelievably hard, but she couldn't have cancelled them; it wouldn't have been fair. She then flew out to see her parents, desperately pretended that all was well with their little girl's world, and five weeks later, tanned, her hair streaked lighter by the Florida sun, she emerged from a taxi outside her house, and even in a cotton T-shirt and loose trousers she looked efficient, in control of her life. A fragile façade, but not an obvious one— or only to someone who knew her very well. She helped the driver carry her luggage up her path, tipped him, and gave a sigh of relief. It was nice to be home. The front garden was a riot of colour—it was also full of weeds, she noted ruefully. Finding her key, she unlocked the door, and hurried to answer the phone.

'Hello?' she said breathlessly.

'Davina?'

'Yes.'

'Well, thank goodness for that! Where on earth have you been?'

'Florida,' she said weakly. 'Who *is* this?'

'Celia.'

'*Celia*?'

'Yes, Celia,' she snorted impatiently, 'and please stop repeating everything I say! I need your help, and trust you to go away just when it's most inconvenient! He's being completely impossible!'

'Who is?'

'Joel, of course!'

Joel? Closing her eyes in defeat, she took a deep breath, and demanded, 'Well, what am I supposed to do about it?'

'Come and see him!'

'And what good will that do?'

'Well, I don't know, do I? But seeing as the whole thing started when you disappeared——'

'I didn't disappear! I went to——'

'Florida, yes, I know,' she broke in impatiently, 'although why you wanted to go there...'

'It's a very nice place——'

'I dare say it is! But I wanted you *here*!'

Totally astonished, Davina held the phone away from her ear, stared at it, then put it back. 'Celia,' she began reasonably, 'I can't live my life the way you want it to be lived. I have commitments of my own.'

'I didn't say you didn't! And stop pretending you don't care. Now, get up here pronto! Hang on, I'll give you the address!'

'Celia,' she said hurriedly before the other woman could disappear, 'I have literally just this second come back! I can't dash off again without a moment's notice—even if I wanted to, which I don't.'

'Yes, you do! Don't be so feeble!' There was a pause, more than a pause, more like a horrified silence before she whispered, 'You didn't go and get *married*, did you?'

'Married? Of course I didn't get married! But I cannot come dashing up to town just because you say so, or because Joel is being impossible! He's *always* impossible!'

'*I* know that and *you* know that, but the investors who are coming to the gallery to see him this afternoon only *suspect* it! And I for one will not stand by and see him throw his career away on a whim—or my livelihood!'

'What whim?'

'He's refusing to attend the exhibition!'

'*What* exhibition?' Davina demanded in exasperation.

'The exhibition of *his* paintings, this afternoon! He *says* he's taking a flying lesson!'

'He's *what*?'

'Taking a flying lesson!'

'But he doesn't fly!'

'Precisely!'

Sinking weakly down on to the stool beside the telephone, the front door still wide open, Davina stared at her luggage tumbled on the step. 'But *why*?'

'I suspect because you ditched him.'

'I didn't ditch him,' she protested, '*he* ditched me!'

'Amounts to the same thing.'

'No, it doesn't.'

'Davina! Just get up here!'

'But he won't take any notice of *me*!'

'He might.'

Oh, this was crazy!

'And I was going to say come here, but I think it would be best to go to his house. How long will it take you? If you come up the A3——'

'Celia, I don't *want* to see him!'

'Stop interrupting. An hour? Hour and a half? That will just give us time. The exhibition starts at five.'

'Celia——'

'Start *now*,' she said firmly, then put the phone down.

Holding the receiver away from her, Davina stared at it somewhat blankly. *Flying* lessons? Was it a joke? And what notice was he going to take of her, for goodness' sake? None. Absolutely none! And she didn't *want* to see him again. She'd just spent the last five weeks trying to *forget* him!

Absently replacing the receiver, she jumped and nearly fell off her stool when it immediately rang. Snatching it up, she barked irritably, 'What?'

'*Now*, Davina,' Celia instructed. 'Now!'

'Oh…' Slamming the phone down, she got up, dragged her luggage inside, and without giving herself time to think grabbed her car keys from the hook above the phone, slung her bag over her shoulder and stormed out.

You're mad, she told herself as she drove towards London. Absolutely stark raving mad! He's treated you like… And what notice is he likely to take of you? None! You're jet-lagged, grubby, hair uncombed, no make-up on, and here you are obediently driving to Ham just because Joel's ex-girlfriend told you to! Absolutely raving bonkers, Davina! Completely out of your tree! Babies have more sense! A lunatic would have more sense!

It took her an hour and a half, and when she pulled up outside his house, still scolding herself for her folly, she just sat there, staring at it, but if she thought she could drive away again unnoticed she reckoned without Celia, who must have been watching for her, because the front door was flung open, then the gate, and she was practically dragged from the car.

'Good girl!'

'Good?' she demanded. 'What's good about it? I must be mad! Or masochistic!'

'Oh, do stop arguing, we don't have much time. He's in the lounge.'

'But what on earth makes you think I can help?'

'Because I know him! At least, as well as anyone ever knows him! And I am not throwing away my future without a fight!'

'Celia,' she tried patiently, 'I don't know what you're talking about.'

With an impatient sigh, obviously someone who absolutely hated having to explain things, Celia said, 'I want to open another gallery, and to do so I need investors. Yes?'

'Yes,' Davina agreed.

'Joel agreed to give an exhibition of his work so that said investors could see how popular he was, how people would rush to buy his paintings, yes?'

'Yes, but——'

'So go in there and persuade him!'

And Joel called *her* bossy? 'But he won't take any notice of me,' she repeated weakly.

'He might. He feels *something* for you at any rate! That day you came he was blisteringly angry.'

'Indifferent,' Davina corrected her, puzzled.

'No, he wasn't; that's the way he is when he's angry and, believe me, I should know; we had enough rows to... Anyway, that's how he goes when he's hurt, or mad, or something. Cool and derisive. Now go and talk to him.'

Digging in her heels, Davina muttered, 'It won't *work*! And why *flying* lessons, for goodness' sake? I don't even know *why* he won't fly!'

Celia sighed. 'He was in a bad air crash last year, said it was a warning not to tempt fate. He dragged some schoolchildren clear; that's when he dislocated his shoulder for the first time. He's always dislocating the wretched thing! *That's* why I was examining it in France.

Helen keeps on at him to get it pinned, but he won't. He doesn't like *hospitals* either.'

'He doesn't like me!'

'Yes, he does!' Without giving her time to argue further, Celia half pushed, half dragged a bewildered Davina inside.

Thrust into the room she'd been in before, tiredness washing over her in waves, Davina surveyed the two occupants—George and a stony-faced Joel. Both men turned at her unorthodox entrance.

'Davina!' Celia announced, as though there might be some doubt.

Both men looked at her, George with a weak smile, Joel with derision. He looked even more dissolute than usual, and Davina felt her heart race.

'Well, well, look who's decided to drop in. How nice of you to come.'

'Oh, shut up,' she retorted wearily, 'and it wasn't *my* idea! For all I care you can go deep-sea diving on Mars——'

'I don't think it has any water,' he drawled.

'Even better; perhaps it will bang some sense into your stupid head.'

'We'll leave you,' Celia said hastily. 'I'm sure you have lots to talk about, but don't be *too* long.' Giving Davina a meaningful look, she added bossily, 'Come along, George.' George meekly went, and left a nasty little silence behind him.

'What are you doing here?' Joel demanded.

'How should I know?' Davina asked defeatedly. 'Celia seemed to think I could persuade you to go to the exhibition.'

'Then Celia has rocks in her head.'

'So I told her.'

'But you still came.'

'Obviously.' And she could be strong, she suddenly realised. She could be indifferent. It might only be an indifference pasted thinly over the armour she'd encased her emotions in, but it seemed to be holding, and that, at the moment, was all that mattered. 'Why don't you want to go?'

'I don't like being fawned over, and I'm certainly not in the mood to listen to a lot of people either praising or criticising, most of whom know absolutely nothing about art!'

'Is that so important? Isn't it allowed just to enjoy? Like or dislike because that's their taste?'

He looked as though he didn't care whether it was or it wasn't, just shrugged. 'Of course it's allowed, but people don't stop at that, do they? They comment on light or shade, texture, brush-strokes as though they actually know what the hell they're talking about.'

'And you're incapable of keeping quiet? Of pretending an interest in what they say? What do you do? Sneer?'

'Why shouldn't I? I painted the bloody things!'

'And presumably want people to buy them.'

'Presumably I do,' he derided, 'but perhaps I look on them as my babies, want them to go to a good home where they'll be appreciated! Isn't that what Freud would have said?'

'I've no idea, I've never read him. I doubt you have either. And goody-goodies are the thieves of virtue,' she tacked on incomprehensibly.

'I beg your pardon?' he asked blankly.

'Nothing, just a quote that popped into my head.' And she had no more idea why she'd said it than he had.

Probably she was cracking up. The oddest things seemed to pop into her head nowadays. 'How's Ammy?'

'Fine. How's Michael?'

'I've no idea; I haven't seen him.'

'Poor Michael.'

'Oh, shut up! I told you he was my editor. *Only* my editor.'

'And you always hurl yourself into his arms, do you?'

'No.'

'And you aren't engaged to him?'

'No.'

'You lied, in fact.'

'Yes.'

'Why?'

'Protection.'

'Protection?' he scoffed. 'From me?'

'Yes. Look, do you mind if I sit down? I'm absolutely whacked.' Walking across to the chair she'd sat in before, what seemed like light-years ago, she collapsed thankfully into the cushions. 'Jet-lagged,' she murmured in explanation. Leaning her head back, she closed her eyes.

'Hence the tan.'

'Mmm. Florida.'

'How are your parents?'

'Fine.'

'Mum's arthritis OK?'

'Mmm.'

'Well, don't go to sleep!' he castigated. 'You're supposed to be here to persuade me to go the exhibition!'

Tiredly opening her eyes, she stared at him, then said quietly, 'Joel, I don't give a damn whether you go to the exhibition or not.'

'Then you should have stayed at home.'

'How true.'

He sighed, shoved his hands into his trouser pockets, leaned his hips against a nearby table. 'Why did you need protection from me? Because you thought I would——?'

'No,' she denied, 'because I thought *I* would. Seeing you again, with Ammy, made me realise what I'd been missing. I suddenly found that I wanted to marry, have children, a little girl maybe...'

'*I* made you see that?' he asked incredulously.

'Yes. It was the way she looked at you, so loving, trusting, not *judging*—and I wanted it for me. Wanted warm little arms to steal round my neck, someone to teach, mould. All the joy...'

'But I'm not...'

She gave a sad smile. 'The marrying kind? I know that; that's——'

'Stop putting words in my mouth.'

'—why I invented a fiancé,' she concluded determinedly.

'A barrier that you hoped I wouldn't cross?'

'Yes.'

'Because of what happened before?'

'Yes.'

'The one barrier that I might respect.'

'Yes. You wanted my body, my—passion, but you didn't want me. Did you?'

'Didn't I?'

'No.'

'And you don't think that your body, warmth, passion *is* you? They can't be separated into components, so that's a shirt that won't wash, but you get an idea, don't you, Davina, and then run with it until either you're exhausted or someone trips you up and brings you down?'

'No, and *you* didn't look past your immediate needs, did you? Your—frustration.'

He gave a derisive smile. 'I'm not a boy, Davina, and, by your own definition of my character, don't you think I knew enough "ladies" to appease my—appetite? Damned if I do and damned if I don't,' he murmured. 'And I no longer affect you, do I?'

'If you ever did.'

There was a little silence. 'Didn't I?'

'Yes,' she muttered.

'But no longer do? Or only pretending I no longer do?'

'Does it matter?'

'Yes.'

'Why? I don't affect you; you said so. You said you were indifferent.'

'Did I?'

'Yes.' But Celia had just said . . . 'Anyway, I knew you weren't in love with me. Knew it was only a short-term thing—although not so short that it would end in Portsmouth!'

'Oh, don't be stupid.'

'Stupid? It was you who said it! In fact you made it quite clear you only wanted my body, and I knew——'

'That when I'd had it I would go on my merry way?'

'You've never been merry,' she derided stupidly.

'And you expect to be rejected, don't you? Even promote it.'

'Rubbish.' But it wasn't. She knew it wasn't. She did expect to be rejected—had, she mentally corrected. Had. But not any more, and she was so tired, she just wanted to close her eyes, go to sleep.

'Is it? Don't you leap in first? Fire off the first salvo?'

'No.'

'Then why the accusations?'

'I was hurt!' she shouted. 'You should have understood that!'

'The way I expected you to understand that I couldn't be, wouldn't be romping on the bed with another woman when only a few hours earlier I'd been romping with you?'

'Perhaps you're over-sexed,' she retorted flippantly.

'Don't be tart; it doesn't suit you.'

'How would you know?'

He gave a cold smile. 'Is that uncertainty I hear in your voice, Davina? Our new-found composure have a little crack, does it?'

'No, it's jet-lag, and even if it weren't it doesn't change anything.'

'Doesn't it?'

'No.'

Staring at him, at his thick dark hair, blue, blue eyes, the barely perceptible scar on the side of his moody face, so tired that his voice seemed to be coming from a great distance, she whispered softly, 'The only man who made me feel like that. The only man there ever was.' She didn't think she'd intended to say it aloud.

'What?' he demanded, and if she'd been in any state to notice she'd have seen he was shocked.

'Nothing,' she denied, 'although I think it was definitely a mistake not to have anyone else.' With a very unhumorous laugh, she added, 'But then, I never wanted anyone else.'

'What? Davina, are you saying...?'

'And I thought it so special,' she murmured with self-denigration. 'Fools come in all shapes and sizes, don't they?' Unable to keep her eyes open any longer, she allowed weighted lids to droop, and in seconds she was fast asleep.

'Davina! Oh, damn you.' He took a step forward, hand out as if to shake her awake, and then thought better of it. Staring down at her, a rather bitter twist to his mouth, a brooding light in his blue eyes, he sighed. 'You screwed up my life, lady,' he told her softly. 'For too many years, you've screwed up my life.'

'Joel?'

Turning only his head, he stared at Celia and, at his most sardonic, drawled, 'I sometimes think, my dear ex-lover, that you don't have a brain.' Hooking up his jacket from the back of a chair, he walked towards the door. 'Well, come on; if we're going to this damned exhibition, let's get it over with—and don't smirk!'

CHAPTER SEVEN

OPENING her eyes, Davina stared at black leather from very close quarters. Squinting, she took several moments to realise that she hadn't the faintest idea where she was, only that she was lying on a black leather sofa. Rolling on to her back, she stared at a room that was both familiar and unfamiliar. And she felt like death. Pushing the light blanket aside, she swung her legs to the floor. Sunlight filtered through tangled vines outside the window. Joel. She'd come to persuade him to go to an exhibition, and had obviously fallen asleep. Great. Depression settled on her like a black cloud. She felt dull and lifeless, and stupid.

Pushing her hair back, she continued to sit, elbows on knees, staring down at the floor. She vaguely remembered a conversation about flying. Appropriate, she supposed dully, for a fallen angel. Glancing at her wrist, she stared at the insect bite that had prevented her wearing her watch. Looking up, she glanced at the mantelpiece. No clock. And the house was silent. Empty. Funny how you could always tell. Had they gone to the exhibition after all? Oh, just get up, Davina, she told herself. Go home. Feeling fatalistic, she nodded to herself, yawned, and got creakily to her feet. She felt a hundred and three.

Finding her shoes, which someone had obviously removed, she wandered out and into the kitchen. Pouring herself a glass of water, she slowly sipped as she stared out into the back garden and absently tried to decide if it was meant to be like that—artistically casual—or whether it was just wild and overgrown, uncared for. Some great master plan, or neglect. Go home, Davina, before he gets back; he doesn't want you here.

Replacing the glass on the draining-board, she collected her bag from the lounge, used the mirror over the fireplace to tidy herself as best she could. She needed a shower, needed a change of clothes, and wasn't going to get either. In which case...

Bye, Joel, she said silently as she walked along the hall—and found that she wanted to cry. No, not just cry. Howl for all the might-have-beens.

'Davina?'

Swinging round, she stared upwards. Joel was perched on the first bend of the winding staircase. A navy towelling robe was insecurely belted around his waist. His forearms lay along his bare knees, hands dangling, bare toes curled over the step below. He looked—special, and such an overwhelming feeling of love flowed over her that she swayed, and if the wall hadn't been behind her she thought she might have fallen. She'd tried to persuade herself that she wasn't in love with him, but she was. So very much, and she almost hated him at that moment for doing this to her. And that heavy weight she'd been carrying around for weeks seemed to settle deeper into her heart. Fatalism.

'You didn't go?' she asked stupidly.

'Go?'

'To the exhibition.'

'Oh, yes, I went.'

'Was it all right? You obviously didn't stay long.' Conversation for the sake of conversation, and because she didn't know how to leave.

'Didn't I?'

'Well, no—at least—I mean, I don't know what the time is.'

'Tomorrow.'

'Pardon?'

'It's tomorrow.'

'What is?'

He gave a slow smile, boyish, appealing, and that wasn't fair. 'Oh, Davina, this is. You slept the clock round.'

Her eyes widening, she exclaimed, 'It's *tomorrow*?'

'Mmm.'

'I'm still in what I wore yesterday?'

He seemed to find that amusing and, his smile softer, warmer, he got to his feet, tightened the belt on his robe, and began to descend. 'The only one?' he queried gently.

'What?'

'You said the only one.'

'Did I? The only one what?' she asked in confusion.

'That's what I want to know.' Reaching her, he rested his hands gently on her shoulders. 'How's your composure this morning?'

It wasn't: she hadn't had time to get it in place. Refusing to look at him, knowing what he might see, she whispered, 'I have to go.'

'Do you?'

'Yes,' she mumbled thickly. 'I have to unpack, open my post...'

'Do you?'

'Yes.'

'The only one?'

And whether it was still jet-lag, waking in strange surroundings or just dammed-up misery her eyes filled, and a lone tear escaped to trickle down her face. 'Oh, Joel, this is no good!' she wailed. 'I have to go *home*!'

Pulling her gently into his arms, he rested his head on hers. 'I sometimes expect,' he said quietly, barely loud enough for her to hear, 'that people I care for should immediately understand, know what I want, feel, without being told.'

'Do you?'

'Yes.'

'You sent me away.'

'I know. I was feeling—ill-used.'

'Did you really believe what I said in Caen?'

'About Michael? Yes, no—hoped,' he explained with a lop-sided smile. 'About the other? No. But you sounded, you see, the way Celia used to sound. Accusatory. And I thought I'd made a very big mistake.'

'Because we were both on shaky ground, I expect.'

Loosing her slightly, he raised her chin so that he could see down into her face. 'Meaning?'

'You're not a man to know, Joel. You make up your own rules.'

'*Everyone* makes up their own rules.'

'No, no, they don't. They might bend them to suit themselves, but you *write* them.'

'Arrogant?'

'Yes. You don't *explain* things. You allow everyone to make assumptions, and when they're wrong you sneer.'

'Do I?'

'Yes.'

'Not a very nice person at all, hmm? Not—lovable?'

'Oh, Joel, of course you're lovable, that's the trouble, but no one ever knows where they stand. There's no feedback.'

'Then what was my loving in France, if not feedback?'

'Desire. Want. Need. You said yourself that it was my face, my body; you didn't say anything about the person inside. You didn't want to *know* the person inside.'

'And did you? Of me?' he asked gently.

'No,' she admitted honestly, 'because I was afraid of what I might see. It all happened so fast, so unexpectedly, and you aren't an easy man to resist.'

'Did you want to resist, Davina?'

'At first, because I knew I'd get hurt.'

'But not later?'

'No.'

'Why?'

'Because I wanted...' Searching his eyes, his strong face, she bit her lip. 'I wanted—the pleasure, the pain, the excitement and warmth. I wanted to pretend that it was—real. Just for a little while. I was—lonely. After Paul—after that party I built a wall around myself, but you knew me before the wall was built, and so, for a little while, I could pretend, and I thought, when it ended, as I knew it would, that I'd be able to put the wall back, or maybe go on to have a relationship with someone else. Only...'

'Only?'

'Only I didn't want anyone else. When I was in Florida, I would look at men, just people passing by in the street, in cars, bars, wherever...' With a big sigh, she shook her head.

'Why did you come yesterday?'

'I don't know. Celia didn't give me time to think. Maybe I thought the wall was safe.'

'And it wasn't?'

'No. Rotten cement, I expect.'

'Too much sand, hmm?' he asked with a faintly wry smile. 'It was a relationship built on memory, wasn't it?

We didn't get to know each other first. Body chemistry without thinking to back it up, and at the first hurdle neither of us was prepared to jump.'

'No.'

'And I blamed you because you made real the something I'd always wanted.'

'What?' she whispered in confusion.

'Never mind, I'll explain later. What did Celia tell you?'

'That you were being impossible.' With a sad smile, she added, 'I can see why you split up, though. She's very—determined, isn't she?'

'Yes, she thinks emotion is a waste of time, that it gets in the way.'

'But not with Ammy, surely?' she began, puzzled.

'No-o, but she's not soft with her—and if she'd been reading her the bird book,' he smiled, 'she would have told her their Latin names, their habitats, not called them Bessie.'

'Ammy told you about it?'

'Mmm. "*Excuse* me"...' His smile gentler, kind, he asked, 'And is that why you came? Because of Celia's determination?'

'No, I don't think so. I think—because I couldn't stay away.'

'And are you saying... *were* you saying, yesterday, before you fell asleep, that you have never been with another man?'

She gave a long sigh, stared at his throat.

'Were you?' he insisted. 'No one? Between that party and now, no one? Davina!' He gave her a little shake, and when she still didn't answer demanded in perplexity, 'Why? It doesn't make sense! I've been sitting there watching you sleep, trying to make sense of i——'

'What? Watching me sleep?'

'Yes, does that bother you?'

Yes, it did. 'You weren't—I mean . . . ?'

'No, when you began to stir, I moved to the stairs. I wanted to know, you see, if you would seek me out before you left or—just leave.'

'I was going to just leave,' she confessed. 'I thought you were at the exhibition.'

'But you didn't want to make sure, just in case?'

'No.'

'Why?'

'Because—you didn't want me.'

'Oh, Davina, any man in his right senses would want you. You're a beautiful, sensuous woman . . .'

'Thank you,' she said drily.

' . . . which makes it doubly hard to understand why there were never any others,' he finished firmly.

'I didn't say I hadn't had any *offers*. Didn't say I hadn't accepted any of them.'

'Your eyes did.'

'Then my eyes lied.'

'Oh, Vina.'

'Don't call me that.'

He gave a funny sort of half-laugh, pulled her against him and rested his head back on her hair. 'Oh, Vina, you're the damnedest woman I've ever met.'

'Yeah,' she mumbled against his robe. And it seemed such a nice place to be. The warmth of him, the gentle rise and fall of his chest. But where did they go from here?

'I find it so hard to believe,' he murmured, as though it had been the sole thing on his mind for the past few minutes.

'Well, don't get too excited,' she muttered tartly. 'I don't intend for it to remain that way.'

He thrust her back, stared at her, and the smile he gave made her extremely nervous. 'But I do.'

'Joel,' she began firmly—well, almost firmly, 'I told you, I want to marry, have a family, be—normal!'

'So?'

'So I'm going home. And, in the words of the late, great Freddy Mercury, I'm going to find me someone to love.'

'You already found him.'

'No, I didn't.'

He smiled, a slow, wolfish smile, and then he picked her up, carried her towards the back of the house, nudged open a doorway, and began to carry her up the secondary staircase towards the bedrooms.

'Put me down! I'm not——'

'Yes, you are.' Laying her on a wide bed, his bed presumably, he unbelted his robe, scolded her gently when she looked away from his nakedness, and then lay beside her. 'And here you are going to stay, until we have discovered all there is to discover about each other. Until you have itemised your life up to the current day, told me your likes, dislikes, your hopes, dreams—and then I will do likewise.'

'No.'

'Yes.'

Swinging her face towards him, almost able to feel the weave of the bedspread through her clothes, the warmth of naked flesh that would soon burn hers, she swallowed hard, shook her head. 'No...' she said hoarsely, her body beginning to respond to his gentle touch as he eased her T-shirt free of her trousers and touched his fingers to her bare midriff. 'No. Anyway, I'm all grubby and I need a shower, clean underwear,' she mumbled half-heartedly.

'You won't need underwear at all,' he grinned, 'but the shower sounds good. Mine,' he added softly. 'All mine.'

'You don't want to marry, have children.'

'Do,' he argued as he began to unbuckle her belt.

'No, you don't. You said... Celia said...'

He paused, looked down into her lovely amber eyes. 'I didn't want to marry and have children with *Celia*,' he corrected her. 'For four, nearly five years you have been my dream. Didn't you know that?'

'You said love didn't exist!'

'Yes,' he agreed, 'because I was so afraid that it didn't, that I would never find it for me.'

'Then why did you never get in touch?' she demanded in perplexity. So much anguish could have been avoided if he had.

'At first because there was Ammy, and although she was conceived in error I did have a responsibility towards her, towards Celia—not that she wanted it,' he added with a wry smile. 'She thought I was fussing unnecessarily. I was born into the wrong age,' he murmured, his smile even wryer. 'I should have been born into an age where women were helpless little creatures who needed protection...'

'I thought you loved her,' she put in quietly.

'No, I told you, only fond, but I did mistake her unutterable certainty in herself, her concern for my welfare, my talent, for commitment to me. Until the certainty became obsession. I can be led, but not pushed.'

'But I didn't think you wanted commitment,' she said, puzzled.

'*You* didn't think. You put a lot of labels on me, Davina. Not all of them were warranted. And I don't think I didn't *want* commitment, I think I was afraid of it. Perhaps, like you, I was afraid of rejection. I've been doing a lot of thinking over the past few weeks, and I've come to the conclusion that maybe I was afraid to love. Not Ammy, because that's unconditional, as hers is for me, but perhaps because of my mother, as you so skilfully pointed out, I was afraid to let anyone too close, and wouldn't admit the reasons because that seemed weak. I'm not given much to self-analysis, but perhaps that's why I only agree to things on my terms. A need to control, not be controlled.'

'You made Celia stay...'

'Not *made*, but yes, made it very clear that that was what I expected, for Ammy to have a proper family upbringing, proper parents, and I expected Celia to want to stay at home, look after her, feel as I felt, because...'

'Because you were an unwanted child, and you didn't want Ammy to grow up feeling as you had felt?'

'Yes, in the beginning anyway, but then—oh, Davina, I loved her so, that little baby. Found that I needed the love she gave me. Unqualified. Adored without reservation. I've always wanted to be loved like that. I assumed Celia did too.'

'But love comes in different guises,' Davina pointed out softly. 'It didn't mean she loved her less just because she wanted to have some independence too.'

'No, I know that now, but it still doesn't seem—right. I didn't understand that Celia felt stifled, that her need to organise was the same as my need to paint. And I didn't force my opinions down her throat, as she tried to force hers down mine until it began to feel as though she wanted to *own* me, body and soul. And so we eventually parted again because I couldn't, wouldn't account for every minute of every day to her.'

'That was why you were so angry in France...'

'Yes, another accounting.'

'And if I hadn't come...'

'I would have come to you, because I couldn't have stayed away—after a suitable interval for punishment, of course.'

'But that's...'

'Calculated cruelty? Yes. I was angry. I'm trying to be honest, Davina. I told you I have a dark side, and I wanted to punish you for doubting me. But revenge is a double-edged sword. I also punished myself. But after I'd gone to all the trouble of finding you in Andor——'

'*Finding* me? You didn't find me, you saw me by... Why are you shaking your head? It was coincidence, fate, whatever...'

'Davina, Davina,' he crooned softly. 'Devera was an excuse. I *knew* you were in Andorra, knew what you were doing there.'

'How?'

'How do you think? You say you kept track of me through the tabloids—do you think I was any less interested when I saw the advertisement for your first book? But I was still with Celia then, so I could only follow with my eyes, not with my heart.'

'Your heart?' she whispered.

'Of course my heart.'

'So if Celia hadn't been pregnant...'

'Yes. If Celia hadn't been pregnant.'

As they stared at each other, both seeing a life that might have been, Davina closed her eyes on a flood of emotion, because her might-have-been was so different from his—and he didn't know, couldn't know... She almost told him about the baby then—almost, but if she did, and he felt as he said he did, it would be a hurt he did not deserve. To withhold the knowledge of her pregnancy would be kinder, a gift he would never know she had given. To tell him would alter nothing, only give more anguish, because nothing could change the past—and so she kept silent. But it was so hard, not to be able to share it. Fighting to compose herself, she managed softly, 'Go on.'

'By one of those quirks of fate, I saw Jackie, that friend who dragged you to that party all those years ago. I don't know if she remembered who I was...'

'Oh, Joel!' she exclaimed helplessly. No one, either young or old, who had ever met him would ever forget who he was.

With a funny little shrug, he continued, 'I asked about you, just casually, you understand, and she told me about the tour, even told me where you'd be. And Devera lived in Andorra, not that far from your own destination, had been on at me for ages to paint his portrait, and so I accepted the commission... The rest you know.'

'And he still hasn't got himself painted,' she said foolishly.

With a delighted laugh, he hugged her to him. 'No,' he agreed, 'he still hasn't got himself painted.' Gently stroking one finger down her cheek, he asked, 'Does it bother you? That Celia's still on the scene, so to speak?'

Thinking about it honestly, and knowing they hadn't even begun to cover the real issues, she said, 'Yes and no. The fact that she knew you, loved you, bothers me...'

'The way that thinking of Michael bothered me? When I saw him come out of your cottage, a place he was obviously used to, where he could come and go at will...'

'No,' she denied, 'he knows I leave the key under the flowerpot, but he doesn't usually come there.'

'I imagined him kissing you,' he continued, 'as I had kissed you, taking you inside, loving you as I had loved you, and I wanted to—kill.'

'But he didn't, wasn't... I quite like Celia,' she said stupidly.

'So do I, sometimes—so long as I don't have to live with her. What did she tell you about me that day you came here?'

'Nothing very much,' she said.

'But enough to send you winging off to Florida?'

'No, she said to let you go hang. Only it was the other way round, wasn't it? You cared so little that you left it at that.'

'No. I came down to see you a few days later, but a woman walking her dog said you'd gone away.'

'I'm surprised you remembered where I lived,' she murmured peevishly as she recalled his behaviour that day.

He smiled, flicked a finger against her cheek. 'Even if I hadn't, I knew your address—from your luggage tag.'

Staring at him, she gave a weak smile. 'So if I hadn't rushed off...'

'Yes, the last five weeks could have been avoided. How did you know where *I* lived?'

'I watched you sign the register in the hotel.'

His smile crinkled his eyes, and he touched his mouth to her exquisite nose. 'I was going to come out to Florida, only then—I—er—dislocated my shoulder again...'

'Joel!'

'And Helen insisted I go into hospital and have it pinned.'

'*How* did you dislocate it?'

'Playing roundabouting with Ammy. I was the round-about,' he admitted ruefully.

'Oh, Joel. Is it all right now?'

He nodded. 'But I think it was the longest five weeks of my life.' Resting his head on his outstretched arm so that his face was beside her own, he murmured, 'When I was a little boy, I used to look in people's windows. Watch the families. A mother and father, children, and I wanted it to be like that for me. I would imagine the fathers playing with the children, watching the television, cosy, intimate, the mother in the kitchen maybe, cooking the dinner—and then I would go home, to a usually empty house, or empty of anyone but the *au pair*, go up to my room, and dream.'

'Oh, Joel. Because your mother wasn't maternal?'

'Mmm. I was an—error.'

'But once she saw you, held you...'

'Apparently not. Just the way she was. Is. She wasn't a bad mother, just different. Her career kept her busy, and I was just a little person who shared her life.'

'And your father?'

'He died when I was three. And because, presumably, she thought it the right thing to do, what all the other mothers she knew did, I went off to boarding-school when I was seven.'

'That's terrible!'

'No, it isn't. It—happens.'

'And if you'd had a son...'

'When I have a son,' he corrected her softly.

A son? A little brother for Ammy? A little baby to hold... Swallowing a rush of emotion, Davina asked carefully, 'Would you have sent him to boarding-school?'

'No.'

'Why?' she asked curiously.

He gave a wry smile. 'Because I hated it.'

Staring into his eyes, imagining him as a little boy, she touched a gentle hand to his cheek. 'Another reason for not leaving Celia and Ammy.'

'Yes. I remembered very vividly growing up without a father, and I didn't want that for Moppet. I thought that my wishes, hopes, dreams had to come second. Do you understand?'

'Yes.' And she did, loved him the more for it. 'I thought you saw me as a challenge, someone to punish for what I had done to you.'

'I know you did.'

'Then why didn't you say?'

'In case it went wrong, in case the dream was faulty, but when I saw you again, travelled with you, saw how you were with Ammy, the need grew, and lying in hospital, even though I was in a private room, I would see wives, children come to visit their husbands, fathers— and I wanted it for me. And so the minute your name came up on the flight list——'

Jerking upright, nearly toppling him to the floor, she echoed, 'Flight list? You *knew* which flight I'd be on?'

'Of course I did. Every Florida flight list for the past few weeks has been scanned.'

'Can you do that?' she asked.

'I can ask if your name is on it. A simple yea or nay is sufficient.'

Still staring at him in shocked surprise, she suddenly accused, 'You *made* Celia ring me.'

He gave a slow smile, then chuckled. 'Celia is quite easy to manipulate once you get her measure. I wouldn't attend the exhibition unless...'

'But why not ring me yourself?'

'Because I didn't want to talk to you on the phone. I needed to see your face, your expression.'

'But when I came you were horrible!'

'Mmm. I have discovered that the only way to make you confess things is to make you angry, and then you blurt them out. What I didn't expect was the blurting I got,' he smiled. 'And before I could capitalise on it you fell asleep.'

'Yes, well...' Suddenly remembering something he had said downstairs, she murmured. 'Made real something you'd always wanted.' A frown in her eyes, she asked hesitantly, 'Joel, are you saying that...?'

'I want to marry you? Yes. That you stayed in my mind as a dream? Yes. And when I met you again it felt—special.'

'But in France, when I caused that scene, you thought you'd made a mistake?'

'Yes. Thought I'd created a perfect person out of flawed goods.'

'Perhaps you did. You don't *know* me.'

'I don't know you very *well*,' he qualified. 'I know some things about you—that you expect the worst, for one thing,' he smiled. 'I know that you're kind, clever, courageous. I know that the knowledge that I've been the only man in your life makes me feel—special. I know that our short time in France together, despite the injuries, was the happiest I've ever spent.'

'Was it?' she asked softly, surprised, and flattered.

'Yes.'

'But you do things on a whim, don't you?'

'Sometimes. According to others, I'm either coldly calculating or whimsical. As the mood takes me. But you're not a whim, Davina.'

'But I still don't understand why you *wanted* to!' she cried in perplexity. '*I* used you! *Told* you I'd used you! I would have expected that if you'd thought about me at all it would have been with disgust! Anger!'

'It was at first, of course it was, but you see, when I began to think about it properly, examine it, I remembered that the expression in your eyes hadn't reflected the expression in your voice, and the more I thought about it, the more I came to understand. And it haunted me,' he said simply.

'Then why didn't you get in touch when you and Celia *did* split up?'

'Because I was in an air crash, and I spent several months in hospital...'

'Oh. Your arm—that was when you first dislocated your shoulder.'

'Yes.'

'I didn't know,' she whispered. 'It was never in the papers...'

'No, it happened abroad, and I deliberately kept it quiet. Looked in the papers often, did you?' he teased.

'No,' she denied with a stiff little expression that made him smile.

'Liar.'

'I sometimes looked in the papers,' she admitted.

'Good. I wouldn't want it to be all one-sided.'

'Celia said you rescued some children...'

'Did she?'

'Yes. How badly were you hurt?'

'Not badly,' he dismissed. 'A few broken bones...'

'A few broken bones don't mean you spend months in hospital!'

'There were—complications,' he admitted wryly. 'Infection, hairline fracture of the skull, things like that.'

'Don't be so dismissive!' she retorted angrily. 'You could have been killed!'

'Could, but wasn't.' Trailing his finger gently down her nose, he added softly, 'But thank you for your concern.'

'I wish I'd been there.'

'So do I. Is the memory still vivid, Davina? Of when we met?'

She looked down, shamed still by her behaviour that day. 'Yes.'

'I'd never felt like that. So—overwhelmed. And what happened in that bathroom...'

'Oh, don't,' she groaned in embarrassment. 'I still can't believe...'

'No, no more can I—an overwhelming passion, just like that. I wasn't thinking when I turned to find you following me upstairs, no plan, no ideas, just a compulsion, and when I took your hand soul met soul, mind met mind. I can see it so clearly, the way you stared at me, reached out for me, and the rest was—heaven. It spoilt me, Davina, gave me a yardstick that no one else ever measured up to—and yet when I found out where you were I was almost afraid... I've found over the years that going back is usually a mistake, and so when I saw you again I was fully prepared—half prepared,' he qualified, 'to feel nothing. To be—disappointed. And I so desperately didn't want to be. But what I wasn't prepared for was the rush of feeling I had when I *did* see you walk into that room. Time unravelled backwards, and I wanted you, just as I had all those years ago. One look, and I wanted you. Not just your body, but your heart and mind, and with a hunger so fierce it was frightening. And that was how you felt, wasn't it?'

'Yes.'

'How you feel now?' he asked softly.

'Yes, but...'

'No buts,' he argued.

'But we don't know each other very well.'

'Yet. What is it that you want from a relationship, Davina?'

'I don't know,' she whispered. 'To be loved, cared for, protected. Someone to laugh with...'

'Someone to trust with your very life?'

'Yes.'

'And don't you think we could have that? I wasn't sure that love existed, that the picture in my mind could ever be a reality, but I learned of the love of a child for her father, learned of my love for her—and I yearned for that special feeling that I'd experienced with a lovely young woman at a party. A brief encounter, because Celia discovered she was pregnant, and I think I almost hated her for that. Until, nearly five years later, I found you again. A lady whose tough exterior hid a vulnerability that made me feel protective, and apart from how you can make me feel emotionally, sexually you're a sweet, funny lady. You won't be a doormat, won't be trodden on, and if you can believe that I love you, and all that it means, then... Are you doubtful because of my failed relationship with Celia?'

She shook her head.

'Even in the beginning, I had never felt as I felt with you, never loved as this is love, otherwise I would have asked her to marry me—although, knowing her as I know her now, I doubt she would have agreed—or only on her terms—and I do so hate being ordered,' he whispered softly. 'But if you asked... Oh, Davina, if you asked.'

Staring into his eyes, feeling her senses beginning to blur, knowing that if she tried to speak her voice would be thick, she gave a shaky sigh. 'Is that all it would take?' she managed huskily.

'Yes, that's all it would take. I *knew* that was all it would take the moment I saw you in Andorra. Standing there, a drink in one hand, I watched you, watched you laugh, smile, lean forward to emphasise some point or another, and I felt my body stir, aroused and aching, a heaviness in my limbs, a drag in my stomach. A linen dress cut on military lines, severe, and it enhanced every curve, drew attention to your full breasts, the flare of your hips, hinted at the promise of curves and hollows, and I wanted to walk across, draw you into the shadows, remove every item of clothing, slowly, oh, so slowly, tangle my fingers in that marmalade hair, and ravish you. I wanted to fill every part of you, touch every part of you, have you boneless and weak—mine.' As he'd spoken his eyes had grown darker, his hands still as they rested, one on her hair, the other at her midriff, and then his eyes moved to her mouth, and as if in slow motion drew nearer until his tongue could touch against her slightly parted lips, and she groaned, stirred, moved her hand to his thigh, felt the warm, smooth flesh, and then gave a long shudder as lips touched lips, as his hand found her full breast, eased her bra aside.

'We belong, Davina,' he murmured huskily. 'We always belonged.'

'But when you came to my apartment in Andorra you were—almost dismissive.'

'Because I was afraid the dream would die. And if I'd told you how I felt you would have laughed in my face.'

'No, I wouldn't.'

'Wouldn't you? But it was a chance I wasn't prepared to take. It was too important to me. And so I pretended I couldn't drive, knowing that kind Davina would offer,' he murmured wickedly.

'Was there a train?'

He nodded, chuckled.

'You *were* pursuing me.'

'Of course I was. Softly, softly, catchee monkey.'

'Rat.'

'Mmm. And then, when I knew I was the only man to touch you, there was nowhere to go but here.' Releasing her breast, he took her hand, led it where he wanted it to lie, gave an ecstatic little shudder, and searched her eyes for her own truth.

'Do you love me?' he asked thickly.

'Yes,' she breathed.

'And we won't accuse, we'll ask. Yes?'

'Yes. Do you love *me*?'

'Yes. I'm an awkward devil, difficult and moody— talented,' he added with a shaky grin. 'And you're mine. Only mine. No one else will ever touch you as I have touched you.'

'No.'

'Do you have any idea how that makes me feel?'

'No.'

'Like the luckiest man on earth, and your voice is all thick, husky, sexy. For me. Because of me.'

'So is yours.'

'Yes. For you. And even though it's still clothed I can see every inch of your body, every freckle, every pore, and in my mind's eye I'm entering you, touching you, feeling your power...'

'Oh, dear God, Joel,' she groaned as she was flooded with sweet warmth.

'And I want to savour this moment for just a while longer. Tell you what we'll do, how we'll do it, how we'll feel...'

Dragging a deep breath into lungs that felt flattened, old, Davina let it out on a jerky sigh, closed her eyes, leaned her forehead against his, breathed in the scent, the sheer masculinity of him. 'Will it always be like this?'

'Yes. I——'

Clattering footsteps suddenly sounded on the stairs, and he jerked in shock.

'Daddy? I'm here!'

'Gordon Bennett!' he exclaimed faintly. 'It's Saturday.'

'Saturday?'

'Yes!' Leaning sideways, he groped on the floor, hastily grabbed his robe and dragged it over his nakedness. Davina scrambled upright, barely had time to adjust her clothing before the bedroom door slammed open to reveal Ammy, Raggedy Ann clasped upside-down in one arm, a beam as wide as the Severn Bridge on her face.

'Vina!' she exclaimed happily, as though she was the very best person she could hope to see. '*Excuse* me! But can I have my worm back?'

'Haven't had no dinner, haven't had no tea,' Davina completed faintly for her as she hastily finished stuffing her T-shirt back into her trousers.

'And I'm very, very hungry!' Ammy concluded triumphantly with her funny little nod.

'Yes,' Davina agreed—and then she began to laugh. All the tension, the hurt and unhappiness, the sheer exuberance of Ammy, went into it and, doubling over, she sank on to the edge of the bed and laughed until she was helpless, until tears ran down her cheeks, and every time she thought she could stop she'd glance at Ammy's beaming smile and start all over again. 'Oh, my. *Excuse me*. Haven't had no dinner...'

'Haven't had *any* dinner,' Joel corrected her solemnly. 'Grammar, Davina, grammar.' But there was a shake in his voice, a laugh waiting to be born.

Raising her head to look at him, she bit her lip and queried softly, 'And every Saturday you have your daughter for the weekend?'

'Mmm,' he agreed wryly.

Peeping at him through a tangle of hair, she managed, 'Deferred seduction?'

'No! Celia?' he roared.

'Yes, dear?' Celia asked helpfully as she appeared behind her daughter.

'Could you...?' he began, then closed his eyes in defeat when she began to shake her head.

'I'm going away for the weekend. Children not allowed.'

'If this is to get back at me for making you ring Davina...'

'Don't be ridiculous, and do please remember that little pitchers have big ears.' Glancing at Davina, she shook her head at her in mock-reproach. 'You must be mad. However...' Bending, she hugged her daughter goodbye. 'Be good for Daddy, won't you?'

'Good,' she nodded, still beaming at the two on the bed.

'I'll see you on Sunday.'

'Sunday,' Ammy repeated obediently, with another firm little nod.

Celia backed out, hesitated, then gave Joel a wry smile. 'I am glad for you. Really. Be happy.'

'Yes,' he agreed gently and, with his slow, devastating smile, added, 'I'd be even happier if...'

She shook her head, gave a little laugh. 'I can't. Honest. Betteringham?' she prompted.

'Oh, hell.' With a disgusted nod, he waved her away, and they heard her clatter down the stairs, laughing.

'Betteringham?' Davina queried.

'Some art society do she goes to each year,' he explained as he continued to watch his still grinning daughter. 'Children not allowed. Hello, Moppet.'

'Bounce?' she asked hopefully.

'Bounce,' he agreed fatalistically.

Satisfaction in every line of her, Ammy sat, dragged off her shoes, and launched herself on to the side of the bed that Davina hastily vacated. 'Be careful,' she intoned, with her little nod. 'Not fall off.'

'No,' Joel agreed ruefully, 'not fall off.'

A sparkle in her eyes, Davina asked hopefully, 'Did you ask Celia if—er—um . . . you know . . . ?'

An arrested expression on his face, he exclaimed, 'Hell, no! It isn't funny!'

'It is,' she laughed. 'Oh, Joel, it is. And if you don't want to wait until Monday, then you'd best start trying to explain to Ammy that she's going to have an extra mummy—and all that it implies.' Walking towards the door, still laughing delightedly, she waggled her finger at him. 'I'm going home to get a change of clothes.'

'Davina! You come right back here!'

'Won't,' she said softly, her smile as wide as Ammy's had been.

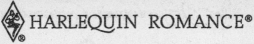

HARLEQUIN ROMANCE®

brings you

The written word has played an important role in all our romances in our Sealed With a Kiss series so far and next month's #3378 *Angels Do Have Wings* by Helen Brooks is no exception.

But just as Angel Murray was writing a long letter to her best friend explaining that nothing exciting ever happened to her—something did. A rich, tall and utterly gorgeous stranger walked into her life and casually turned it upside down.

What could a man like Hunter Ryan possibly want with a girl like her? Despite the attraction that flared between them, they were worlds apart. Angel could never reconcile herself to a temporary affair and that was clearly all he was offering her. But Hunter's charm was proving all too persuasive. And as for his kiss...

From the celebrated author of
And the Bride Wore Black.

SWAK-7

PRIZE SURPRISE
SWEEPSTAKES
OFFICIAL ENTRY COUPON

This entry must be received by: AUGUST 30, 1995
This month's winner will be notified by: SEPTEMBER 15, 1995

YES, I want to win the Wedgwood china service for eight! Please enter me in the drawing and let me know if I've won!

Name_____

Address _____ Apt. _____

City   State/Prov.   Zip/Postal Code

Account #_____

Return entry with invoice in reply envelope.

© 1995 HARLEQUIN ENTERPRISES LTD.   CWW KAL

PRIZE SURPRISE
SWEEPSTAKES
OFFICIAL ENTRY COUPON

This entry must be received by: AUGUST 30, 1995
This month's winner will be notified by: SEPTEMBER 15, 1995

YES, I want to win the Wedgwood china service for eight! Please enter me in the drawing and let me know if I've won!

Name_____

Address _____ Apt. _____

City   State/Prov.   Zip/Postal Code

Account #_____

Return entry with invoice in reply envelope.

© 1995 HARLEQUIN ENTERPRISES LTD.   CWW KAL

OFFICIAL RULES
PRIZE SURPRISE SWEEPSTAKES 3448
NO PURCHASE OR OBLIGATION NECESSARY

Three Harlequin Reader Service 1995 shipments will contain respectively, coupons for entry into three different prize drawings, one for a Panasonic 31" wide-screen TV, another for a 5-piece Wedgwood china service for eight and the third for a Sharp ViewCam camcorder. To enter any drawing using an Entry Coupon, simply complete and mail according to directions.

There is no obligation to continue using the Reader Service to enter and be eligible for any prize drawing. You may also enter any drawing by hand printing the words "Prize Surprise," your name and address on a 3"x5" card and the name of the prize you wish that entry to be considered for (i.e., Panasonic wide-screen TV, Wedgwood china or Sharp ViewCam). Send your 3"x5" entries via first-class mail (limit: one per envelope) to: Prize Surprise Sweepstakes 3448, c/o the prize you wish that entry to be considered for, P.O. Box 1315, Buffalo, NY 14269-1315, USA or P.O. Box 610, Fort Erie, Ontario L2A 5X3, Canada.

To be eligible for the Panasonic wide-screen TV, entries must be received by 6/30/95; for the Wedgwood china, 8/30/95; and for the Sharp ViewCam, 10/30/95.

Winners will be determined in random drawings conducted under the supervision of D.L. Blair, Inc., an independent judging organization whose decisions are final, from among all eligible entries received for that drawing. Approximate prize values are as follows: Panasonic wide-screen TV ($1,800); Wedgwood china ($840) and Sharp ViewCam ($2,000). Sweepstakes open to residents of the U.S. (except Puerto Rico) and Canada, 18 years of age or older. Employees and immediate family members of Harlequin Enterprises, Ltd., D.L. Blair, Inc., their affiliates, subsidiaries and all other agencies, entities and persons connected with the use, marketing or conduct of this sweepstakes are not eligible. Odds of winning a prize are dependent upon the number of eligible entries received for that drawing. Prize drawing and winner notification for each drawing will occur no later than 15 days after deadline for entry eligibility for that drawing. Limit: one prize to an individual, family or organization. All applicable laws and regulations apply. Sweepstakes offer void wherever prohibited by law. Any litigation within the province of Quebec respecting the conduct and awarding of the prizes in this sweepstakes must be submitted to the Regies des loteries et Courses du Quebec. In order to win a prize, residents of Canada will be required to correctly answer a time-limited arithmetical skill-testing question. Value of prizes are in U.S. currency.

Winners will be obligated to sign and return an Affidavit of Eligibility within 30 days of notification. In the event of noncompliance within this time period, prize may not be awarded. If any prize or prize notification is returned as undeliverable, that prize will not be awarded. By acceptance of a prize, winner consents to use of his/her name, photograph or other likeness for purposes of advertising, trade and promotion on behalf of Harlequin Enterprises, Ltd., without further compensation, unless prohibited by law.

For the names of prizewinners (available after 12/31/95), send a self-addressed, stamped envelope to: Prize Surprise Sweepstakes 3448 Winners, P.O. Box 4200, Blair, NE 68009.

RPZ KAL